# THE DESCENDANT

CHRISTIAN MARK

*The Descendant*
Copyright 2019 by Christian Mark

All rights reserved. This is a work of fiction. All characters and places herin are fictitious, even when based on real historical events. No part of this book should be taken as factual historic record.

ISBN: 978-1-950381-15-9

Printed in the United States by
Piscataqua Press
32 Daniel St., Portsmouth, NH 03801

www.ppressbooks.com

This book is dedicated to all the members of the United States Military, their families, and members of all the worlds security services of elected Democratic Republics. Their selfless devotion to protect us, and other countries from evil forces that will always exist in this world. All the authors royalties from this book will go to the Bothers In Arms Foundation, which is a non profit organization supporting Marine special operations community MARSOC, Marine Force Reconnaissance companies, and Reconnaissance Battalions. The foundation will provide financial and logistical assistance to wounded, ill, injured, and fallen operations Marines, sailors, and their families. The address is 3200 South Congress Ave. suite 203, Boynton Beach FL. 33426 PH:855-561-0321

# FOREWORD

Berlin, Germany: 1 May 1945 10:00 P.M.

Negotiations had broken down with the outside world on that final day. Meanwhile, preparations were being made in the Reich Chancellery for the remaining personnel to make an all-out attempt to escape to the West. SS Brigade Leader Monke led the first group from the Bunker. It included Hitler's Adjudent Gunsche, Ambassador Hewel, Vize-Admiral Voss, three of Hitler's secretaries, and a cook.

The second group was led out by Obersturmbundfuhrer Kempka, who brought them up out of the Friedrichstrasse subway station but decided to wait in a theater called the "Admiral's Palace" before trying to cross the River Spree.

At two o'clock, they cautiously came out of the theater and saw a group of people approaching them in the darkness. It was led by Reichsleiter Martin Bormann, dressed in an SS-Gruppenfuhrer uniform. This group included Dr. Naumann, Dr. Stumpfegger, Rach, Schwagermann, Axmann, SS Standartenfuhrer Beetz (one of Hitler's pilots), and two bodyguards.

Bormann was looking for a tank to help break through Russian lines. Just then, three German tanks and three armored personnel carriers moved out of the darkness. Kempka halted the first vehicle.

He ordered the driver to proceed slowly toward Ziegelstrasse and informed him that his group would follow behind with cover. Bormann and Naumann walked to the left of the tank with Kempka behind it.

Suddenly, there was a volley of Russian tank fire exploding all around them. The German tank fired back with one last barrage of shell fire. The tank near Kempka exploded and a huge flame shot out of it. Both Bormann and Naumann were blown aside. The last desperate effort to continue the Thousand Year Reich had failed; only a few had gotten through to freedom.

# Chapter 1

The concussion from the firing Russian tanks had apparently fogged Bormann's head as they made their way on their most glorious mission. Hans and Max had been right at his side throughout the bombardment of shattering metal.

Noise of this nature never seemed to affect them to any degree. Both of them had been with him over the last three years or so, around the Reich Chancellery, and both men had been handpicked for that duty by Heinrich Himmler himself. Even with that aside, Bormann respected the two men and trusted them with his life.

There were rumors that both Hans and Max had been stationed at Auschwitz Extermination Camp in Poland. In the spring of 1941, Himmler was making a tour of all death camp facilities in Poland to determine the expansion that would be needed in order to reach the "Final Solution," the name given to the complete extermination of the Jewish race. Hans and Max were on their regular duties around camp which consisted mostly of degrading and antagonizing the Jewish population.

As it turned out, at the same time Himmler was being escorted around camp by Captain Rudolf Franz, who had been transferred to Auschwitz the previous year. As Himmler was approaching Hans and Max, Max ran up to a young Jewish girl who happened to be passing with her child tucked neatly in her arms. Max seized the child from the screaming mother's arms and proceeded to run up to an outer wall of one of the crematory ovens. Max wound up as if to throw a ball and heaved the little baby headlong into the wall. The blow instantly killed the child. The hysterical mother was on Max's back by then, in a state of shock, trying to kick, bite, and scratch him. He flung her from his body and threw her to the ground. Hans, who had been close to the skirmish, ran up as the woman went for Max again. Hans opened fire with his machine gun, splattering her body into the muddy ground.

Himmler was so intrigued with the ferocity and terror these two men inflicted, he immediately had Captain Franz turn them over to him. They were brought back to Berlin in his own personal staff car and turned over to SS-Obergruppenfuhrer Josef Dietrich for training in the Leibstandarte-SS Adolf Hitler. After their training, they were assigned to guard the Fuhrer and Martin Bormann.

Bormann became quite attached to the two men. He supposed some of it was that of fright because of their bizarre acts of violence that did not even curl a hair on their heads, but also because they put up with him on his worst days at the Reich Chancellery.

Max was a rather tall, thin fellow with brown hair and a very outstanding red scar running from his left ear to the side of his nose. He was an odd person, never really saying much—the coldness that was portrayed from his eyes did all the talking that was needed.

Hans, on the other hand, was quite the opposite. He was very tall with big, broad shoulders and the biggest feet Bormann had ever seen—almost twice the size of Bormann's shoe. Hans loved to joke and was always on hand with something humorous to say to Bormann to cheer him after he had had a bad day, or if the Fuhrer had been in bad spirits which, in turn, saddened Bormann.

Bormann could remember one day after Himmler had gone to see the Fuhrer on some matter of little importance as usual. Bormann was very upset and had been noticeably rude to Hans. Hans stopped and said, in a jubilant sort of voice, "Herr Bormann, do you know what I recently heard?"

Bormann answered sharply, "What?"

Hans continued, "Over thirteen thousand Jews were killed yesterday at Auschwitz. That might be some sort of record, don't you think, Sir?"

"How do you know this news so fast, Hans?"

"My friend, Rudy Roffe, who was stationed at Auschwitz with me for over a year, called me today. He said so many Jews are dying that the men cannot dig the graves fast enough. He also said that their new trick is to have the Jews dig their own grave with shovels until it gets nice and deep. Then they surround the hole and open fire on them with their machine guns until every last Jew is dead."

This delighted Bormann to the utmost. He said, "Hans, at this rate, we shall soon be rid of those meddling fools once and for all. At least something in this Empire runs efficiently. When all is done and everything has been accomplished, things will run like that all over Europe."

13 May 1945

Bormann looked around him through the smoke and noticed that nobody was visible. Everyone was either gone or dead.

Hans turned to him and calmly said, "Herr Reichsleiter, we should be moving on in order to reach our destination as quickly as possible."

Bormann agreed.

Hans was carrying a green duffle bag which contained civilian clothes, false identification papers, money, a compass, food for several days, and three lugers with many clips of ammunition. Changing as quickly as possible, they made their way cross country.

The men had hitched several rides along the way and were now some ten kilometers outside Munich. Having been briefed before the end came close in Berlin, Hans and Max knew exactly where they were going. During the daytime hours on their journey, they slept in the woods or in abandoned farm laborers' cottages. It had been a trying thirteen-day trip, but Bormann was not as tired as he had thought he would be. He reasoned that maybe his body was so tired that he felt rested, as sometimes happened around the Reich Chancellery after a long couple days at work.

They followed a back road leading into Munich for quite some time, trying to avoid Allied patrols which were stopping everyone to ascertain that their papers were in order and not letting any "Nazi criminals," as they called them, out of the country to freedom.

As they walked, Bormann noticed a little farmhouse ahead of them which appeared to be abandoned. Hans and Max stopped for a moment. Max pulled his map out of his pocket to examine his coordinates, then checked his compass. He looked at Bormann confidently and said, "Reichsleiter, we have arrived at our destination."

"Are you absolutely sure, Max?"

"According to my coordinates, this is the correct location."

They approached the farmhouse with caution in case it was inhabited. Their lugers were cocked and ready.

Hans and Max led the way as Bormann brought up the rear. The palms of his hands were beginning to perspire as they crept closer and closer. He had to keep regripping his luger in order to avoid dropping it.

They continued toward the farmhouse until they were up against the south wall of the barn. They crawled on their hands and knees around the corner and up to the door. Hans opened the door ever so slightly with the tip of his gun, then put the toe of his boot in, and with one huge thrust, kicked it open. He stood there for a moment, looking relieved while leaning against the outer wall. From his pocket he retrieved a small, circular red disc about ten centimeters in diameter.

He grasped it in his hand, then threw it into the barn. They waited for a few seconds, then the red disc flew out the door and landed on the ground. They all felt quite relieved knowing they were at their destination.

Bormann then heard a voice say, "Herr Bormann, you are a very prompt man."

He turned to look inside the barn and, to his surprise, saw just one man standing there in civilian clothes with a machine gun pointing in their faces.

"Herr Bormann, promptness is a good virtue, don't you agree?"

"Yes, I agree," he replied quickly. Bormann walked around the man looking at him for some sort of clue as to his name, but he was not familiar at all. He finally asked him in order to be absolutely sure.

"Your name, Soldier?"

He shouted, "OSS Obersturmfuhrer Karl Fritzche, Sir."

"You follow orders very well, Soldier."

"Thank you, Sir," he replied.

"Is the package here?"

"Yes, Sir."

The soldier walked over behind a horse stall and lifted a white bassinet containing a little baby.

"Isn't he handsome, Sir?"

"Yes. He has a true Aryan look about him."

The baby boy was approximately six months old with bright blue eyes and black hair that had a brilliant shine to it. He had a birthmark on his forehead which identified the "package" to Bormann.

Max walked from the barn door which he was guarding and reached into his bag for a bundle of straps which could be put together in order to carry the baby on the second leg of the journey.

Karl was enjoying tickling the baby and making him smile.

All of a sudden they heard a person say, "Don't move! "

Bormann abruptly turned toward the door and saw an American soldier holding a gun on the three of them. He was still outside the barn. Hans, who had been out of his line of sight, just inside the door, stopped breathing. The soldier looked very scared and unsure of what he had stumbled on to. He stood looking at them, his clothes very dirty and his helmet tipped up to his forehead as if it were too big for him.

Hans looked scared standing there silent, as if he did not know what to do. He quietly put his left hand down to his side, bent his knees slightly to remove a bayonet from his boot, then returned to his previous position.

The American started walking hesitantly through the door and then stopped for a moment, making sure not to take his eyes off them for a second. He then continued walking toward them, but before he could finish his next step, Hans wheeled around and knocked the soldier's gun upward with his left hand while thrusting the knife into his stomach with the other. A horrified look came into the soldier's eyes as Hans kept driving the bayonet up into his chest cavity, not easing for a second. The soldier stood there, gasping for air, helpless as to his destiny. After a few seconds, his eyes closed and Hans withdrew the bayonet, letting him fall to the dirt.

"Hans," Bormann yelled, "do you know how important this mission is to the survival of the Thousand Year Reich?"

Hans responded meekly, "Yes, Herr Reichsleiter."

"Then get over by the door and watch outside, and don't take your eyes off the surrounding area. Do you understand, Hans?"

"Yes, Herr Reichsleiter."

Bormann's heart was still pounding from the fright of almost being captured by the enemy and the thought of their mission being lost. He was sorry he had reprimanded Hans, but stupid mistakes in judgment they could not afford.

Bormann decided that this was enough excitement for one day and told everyone to bed down for the night. He felt that the rest would do them more good than anything else. There remained a long and treacherous journey to freedom ahead of them since they had still to tackle the mountains.


21 May 1945


They were very careful on the second part of their journey. Karl was left behind since he carried forged papers that would get him out of the country. Bormann had decided that the less people with them, the better chance they would have of getting through, which was their main goal.

This time the address on their sheet was a house numbered 153, in the village of Nauders situated above the Reschen Pass. It was close to the point where the frontiers of Switzerland, Austria, and Italy met.

Their difficulties in getting there were greater than before, but when they arrived, they learned that Number 153 was the home of one of Austria's best mountain guides, Rudolf Blaas, who had been nicknamed Der Berggeist, "The Phantom of the Mountain," since he had helped hundreds of men cross the frontier illegally. He was politically safe, having acted as a guide for a number of Nazis who had wished to enter Austria just before the Anschluss in 1938.

Mr. Blaas was a pleasant man in his early forties. He was not very talkative, but they realized the less they knew about each other, the better.

Hans and Max were somewhat uneasy around Blaas, but Bormann dismissed this as just being part of their general makeup. Having been in the Leibstandarte-SS Adolf Hitler, they were trained to be suspicious of everyone, even family members.

The little baby was doing well throughout their grueling journey. He had a slight cold, but it was nothing serious. He was a pleasant baby, hardly ever crying, and always seemed to have a smile on his face. Bormann was proud to be carrying the baby with him on their journey.

They remained at Mr. Blaas's house for a couple of days to rest. On the third day they crossed the frontier by way of the Brenner Pass. The steep mountainous terrain was very difficult to cross. Mr. Blaas knew the easiest possible way through the area, which also avoided the frontier guards who seemed to be everywhere.

Several days later they arrived in the town of Merano, Italy, without incident. Mr. Blaas was well paid for his trouble, but they asked him one more favor before they dismissed him. That was to show them to the house of Joseph Wolf. He was the last link in their chain to flee Europe.

26 May 1945

Mr. Joseph Wolf was a member of the Sicherheitspolizei (security police) and assistant to Ernst Kaltenbrunner, head of the department. During the war, Wolf had taken part in a scheme to flood money markets of the world with forged pound notes. His plan, though, had been relatively unsuccessful.

Mr. Wolf was very happy to see them and was well aware of how important this mission was to all members of the Third Reich. They exchanged casual greetings and were then put quickly into the trunk of a specially built car which would be their home for the final two hours they would spend in Europe.

It was a strange trip for Bormann, racing down the mountains in the trunk of a car, although he felt very safe as to Mr. Wolf's competence as a good driver.

Arriving in Venice toward midafternoon, they immediately drove to the dock and passed through security with ease. Mr. Wolf pulled up to the end of the dock and stopped. Bormann heard some discussion and then Mr. Wolf opened the door of the car and got out.

He must have been presenting the order form for the car. There seemed to be something wrong. He heard Mr. Wolf's voice rise to a loud tone.

"Listen, Sir, I have the bill of sale for one 1945 blue Mercedes. I also have the order form here, filled out by Senor Hernandes of Sao Paulo, Brazil. Here are my passport and identification papers ... what more do you want?"

"But Mr. Wolf, my instructions are to always search any car thoroughly that is to be shipped out of the country. It could mean my job if I were to be seen overlooking this duty of mine."

"Listen, Sir," Wolf yelled, "do you know who Senor Hernandes is?"

"No," the man answered in a meek voice.

"Well, he's a very influential, rich, business tycoon in Brazil, with many important friends and political contacts. So maybe you might be disciplined a bit by your superior for overlooking this car, but then again, I can guarantee if there is any further delay, it will mean your job for sure because Senor Hernandez isn't one to be fooled with."

Bormann's heart was in his mouth as to what the result of the argument would be. Their whole mission had come right down to this moment. He waited, knowing that in seconds he would know the outcome.

All of a sudden, he heard a sound. What was it? His heart was pounding louder than he had ever imagined it could.

Then a relieved feeling came to his body. The sound he had heard was that of a crane mechanism being attached to the car in order to load it onto the cargo ship. The ship would bring them to freedom, and their final destination.

Even though there was little light in the trunk of the car, Bormann's eyes had become adjusted to the darkness and he could see Hans's and Max's faces. They each had a grin as wide as the car itself.

He looked at the baby and noticed he was sleeping soundly.

For a short moment, Bormann thought back to those final days of the war when he knew all was lost. He had instructed his wife to flee Berchtesgaden and go to a hiding place in the Tyrol that had been previously chosen. She was to pose as a director of a group of displaced children. He had kidnapped several children which were added to their own in order to make the group look more realistic. Dearly Bormann hoped she had made it to safety. If she were grabbed by Allied forces, they would inevitably torture her in order to find out his whereabouts—but she could tell them nothing.

The car was finally loaded on board and he could hear the steam whistle blowing loudly, which signaled the boat pulling away from the dock. They were leaving Europe and his native homeland for many years. If their mission was successful, however, the Thousand Year Reich would continue someday, not to be conquered ever again.

## Chapter 2

Manhattan, New York          19 June 1983

Simon sat tapping a pencil rhythmically on the kitchen table while staring out the window. He had a rather troubled look on his face, one which I had seen many times before. Simon seemed to enjoy sitting at the table looking out across Manhattan when we were home. Sometimes he would just sit there for hours and stare. From time to time I would ask him what he was looking at. He would just say, "I'm admiring the view, Saul."

The past few weeks had been spent relaxing at home. Simon seemed to think that he could not rest until every Nazi criminal was either in jail or dead.

My view differed just a bit on this subject. My vengeance and determination to succeed in our mission of justice was just as strong as Simon's, but I would not kill myself by neglecting to get my proper rest. I did not mind spending my life capturing and bringing these people to justice, but Simon and I were not getting any younger.

It was an overcast day in Manhattan, but no rain had fallen yet. The view was restricted from our high elevation. I could never understand why he had picked the penthouse of a high-rise apartment building in which to live.

I really shouldn't complain, I thought, the apartment was not costing us anything. Simon's sister, Itka, paid for the apartment and also supported us. Itka was one of the best orthopedic surgeons that Bellevue hospital had ever seen. Simon always bragged about her and how much more intelligent she was than he. After World War II, the newly formed state of Israel paid for her to attend Harvard University School of Medicine in Boston. She was a bright student, graduating eighth in her class. After she passed her medical boards, she came to New York City to practice medicine.

Simon and I had been friends as long as I could remember. Our first meeting was in an alley in Radom, Poland, in 1936. I was being chased by some Gentile boys in town after they had lost a soccer game in which I was the leading point scorer. I ducked down an alley, which I soon knew was a big mistake—it had no exit. They were on me in a second. Two of my offenders held me by the arms while the others punched me in the face. As I remember it, things were starting to go black when out of nowhere another boy charged them with mighty speed, knocking them to the ground. One by one he sorted the boys out, beating them brutally. After the boys had stumbled away totally bruised, he turned to me and said, "Are you all right?"

I responded with a groggy, "Yes."

He introduced himself as Simon Liebmann, a son of a local cobbler. We exchanged hellos, and then walked home together. From that day on, we have been at each other's side.

We both came from relatively poor families living in the ghettos of Radom. At that age, being poor did not bother us as long as we could get out and play after school.

My father was a stern man, standing very tall with big, broad shoulders, and I was always a little afraid of him. His job was that of a loading dock worker for one of the local factories. He always felt you had to work hard in order to live an honest and full life.

My mother lived by the same philosophy. The house was always spotless, and she would always make sure that my father's lunch was ready in the morning. She was a good mother, and I suppose the two of us were closer because we conversed more with each other; my father was never one for words.

At times, I would think back to those awful days when the Germans took over in 1939. The morale in the neighborhood was very low and each day brought more of the unjust beatings plus mass arrests. People became very distant at this time. The main function of everyday life was to avoid arrest and somehow stay alive.

Some families fled to the Soviet Union for comfort, but awful stories were filtering back saying people were being robbed and murdered in the streets.

Finally the day came when we were shipped off to a work camp. The order had been given the night before by a Gestapo major walking down the street. We were to assemble at Fraugut Square with our families and bring whatever we could carry for the trip. My parents had no choice but to obey the orders.

I saw Simon and his family at the formation site; we conversed for a short time, but then were herded into freight cars. A sense of doom came over us as the doors slammed shut. Most of us had to stand very close together, but a few lucky people were able to sit. As the train raced along, we looked through the barred windows and saw villages and sometimes a bridge that had been bombed out.

The first stop was a camp that was many kilometers from home. There the Germans had established a network of making shoes, textiles, and various other articles. The workers were all deported Jews.

The camp itself was heavily guarded with a large wall surrounding the camp and guard towers at all four corners manned with machine guns.

The treatment was far from hospitable. Most guards would go out of their way to make our lives miserable. There was verbal abuse, as well as whippings and beatings. One crucial point to remember, in order to stay alive, was to never hit a German guard. If this happened, our lives would be worth nothing.

My mother and father became very introverted while they were there, not saying much, and sometimes I would feel that my family life had ceased to exist.

Simon's parents had become quite the same. They walked around camp in their spare time not caring about life as much as they had before.

Simon, Itka, and I stuck together very closely, always looking out for one another. The main thing that kept us going was hate for the Germans. We would not let the Germans beat us down to bewildered zombies.

In the spring of 1942, we were taken by train further west through Germany. The trip took several hours. I had a bad feeling inside as to what was to become of me and my family. The outcome was worse than I could ever have expected.

We arrived at a railroad crossing where many trucks were waiting. This is where my life ended for a while. My parents, as well as Simon's parents and many other older folk, were loaded in the trucks. They vanished down the road in a matter of minutes. That would be the last time I would ever see them. I will never forget the look on Itka's face as her mother was ripped from her arms and thrown into a waiting truck. The rumor that had spread through the crowd was that they were taken to an Extermination Camp. The way things were, I really could not doubt that it was the truth.

The younger people, which also included Simon, Itka, and myself, were brought by truck to a nearby ammunitions factory. The work was very hard with horrible conditions, but in the state we were in, it hardly mattered. We worked sixteen hours a day and slept for eight hours. We learned that the trick to working in the factory was not to stop for a moment, and to never get sick. This could mean your life.

## The Descendant

We spent the duration of the war working in the factories, until the Allies liberated them in 1945. Soon after the war was over, Itka decided to go to Palestine where many Jewish survivors were emigrating. We were sad to see her go, but it was something she wanted to do.

Simon and I were lucky enough to join up with a group of Jewish men who ran a documentation center for German war crimes, working out of Vienna. Simon said that he could never rest another day until every Nazi criminal had been captured and punished. The job was very rewarding and consisted mainly of interviewing Jews who had eyewitness testimony of crimes that Nazis had performed in their presence. The people came from all over Central and Eastern Europe to tell their horrible stories.

We had a very complete catalogue of criminals in the Gestapo, SS, and various other military ranks. A lot of people signed sworn documents that could be used in trials against captured Nazis about to come to justice. The rest of the information was used to keep up to date the whereabouts of Nazi criminals, in order that the groups of Jews who hunted them would have a better chance to make the capture.

My heart went out to all the people who entered the center. The average person would enter the building with their identification numbers burned in their wrists and sadness in their eyes. They would tell their story for a while, then break down into tears. It hurt so much because it reminded me of my own parents the day they were taken away.

One of the most horrible stories I heard had been carried out in Russia. The SS and Gestapo units were sent into many cities to shoot all Jews who had fled eastward into central Russia. The order came from Himmler himself and was very explicit. No mercy was allowed. Little Jewish children were literally hurled into the air and shot with bullets. Also, many communist leaders in the cities were hanged in the public square, with the civilian population compelled to watch.

I continued for a couple of years working with Simon there. We were living in a modest house in one of Vienna's outer suburbs. It was very well guarded by husky dogs, which were part of the security system. Also, we both carried pistols at all times, since some Nazi underground organizations did not take too kindly to our line of work.

One day after an interview, Simon walked briskly across the room to his desk and said, "Saul, we are going to join a group of Jews who hunt down these insane killers we hear about every day. I can't stand to just sit here while I know these people are out there and free."

I was not very surprised at his decision to do this, but I wondered what had stirred him up all of a sudden. So, I asked him why, and now wish I never had. Simon pulled a crumbled picture from his pocket, straightened it out, and tossed it on the desk. It showed a naked Jew who was hanging dead from a meat hook by his penis. I instantly felt a rumbling feeling come to my stomach, as if a volcano were ready to erupt. I made a fast exit to the men's room. From that day on, we started to hunt down Nazi criminals.

This sort of life agreed with Simon. He was one of the best Nazi hunters, and probably the most devoted. We spent hour after hour reviewing records and planning strategy, hoping that one of the endless sources of information would give us enough to produce a capture. I had to push myself some of the time to keep up with Simon. I think even if I had stopped what we were doing, Simon would have kept going with his mission.

Our lives consisted of catching planes to many far away countries to investigate the smallest lead.

Probably the most difficult part of the job was slipping into foreign countries, coordinating the commandos to plan a capture, and successfully getting out alive with the prisoner. Many foreign countries sympathized with Nazi war criminals, and this made the job even more complex.

Over the years many nearly successful captures were spoiled by local authorities interfering in our affairs. Some of our key agents were thought to have perished because of local officials conspiring with Nazi criminals. On several occasions, we sent a fellow comrade on a scouting mission to verify the whereabouts of a suspect, and he was never heard from again. These people were highly trained in their occupations, and both Simon and I felt the Nazis had to have more help than we were aware of.

Our record of capture was one of greatness.

Simon and I, plus other commandos who had worked with us occasionally over the years, were proud of the effort and success we'd had with captures. Simon always admitted to great satisfaction in seeing one of these rats brought to justice.

One of the most memorable captures was that of Adolf Eichmann in May of 1960. He was one of the worst enemies to the Jewish people, having been directly responsible for the deportation of millions of Jews to extermination camps all over Germany and Poland.

Eichmann had been in Argentina since the end of World War II under the alias of Ricardo Klement. We obtained information from various legitimate informants that he was working at a Mercedes Benz factory at Suarez, not far from Buenos Aires. We also knew that he was living in the town of Tucuman.

Eichmann was a man of vast suspicion, so the mission had to be conducted with pinpoint accuracy. Before attempting this capture, we wanted to make sure beyond any doubt that the man we were dealing with was really SS Oberstlirmbann-Fuhrer Adolf Eichmann.

Three Israeli agents were sent to discover if Ricardo Klement was in fact Eichmann. They moved into a villa opposite Eichmann's and took pictures of him with a telescopic lens as he exited and entered his home. These pictures were sent to the documentation center in

Haifa, Israel, and were verified to be Adolf Eichmann.

The second phase of the operation was the capture itself. Simon, myself, and two Argentinians were in charge. After we arrived in Buenos Aires, we made contact with our two informants at the airport, who took us to their villa not far from the Eichmann home. We pooled our information at once and set up a plan, deciding to grab him at 6:30 P.M. as he was returning home from work. We rented a car under an alias. I had printed identification cards at the documentation center to verify our names.

I parked the car near the spot where the bus would stop to let Eichmann off. The two other men plus Simon were hiding in the bushes not far from the bus stop. My heart was pumping very fast, and my hands were sweating with anticipation of what was to happen.

Just then a bus pulled up in front of me and stopped. I almost could not believe our luck—only one person stepped off the bus. It was Adolf Eichmann. I was so astonished that I almost leaned on the car horn by mistake.

The bus pulled away and the man began to walk. As he came to the entrance of the path that led to his house, he removed a flashlight in order to see. Before he could turn it on, all three men sprang from the bushes and wrestled Eichmann to the ground. Simon literally shoved his hand into Eichmann's mouth and ripped his false teeth out, which contained a cyanide pill to kill himself in the event this should ever happen. Meanwhile, I pulled up right in front of the scuffle. Simon and one of the other men thrust him into the back seat onto the floor. Adolf Eichmann was captured and we successfully smuggled him back to Israel by plane to stand trial.

We were congratulated in person by the Prime Minister of Israel and reporters buzzed around for weeks, wanting to know every last detail of our lives, and of course, the capture itself. We were glad that this affair was getting so much publicity. It attracted attention to the fact that what we had done was very important and also needed funding to be carried out.

Not long after this event, Simon received word from his sister, Itka, in New York that she was very lonely for him and wished he would move to Manhattan and carry out his affairs from there. After several weeks, we decided to move. We moved from Vienna to Manhattan with a short stop in Haifa to copy all the records on Nazi criminals we would need in order to continue our job in America.

Simon abruptly rose from the kitchen table with an angered look on his face. He proceeded to toss the *New York Times* at the sliding glass door which led to the balcony.

"God dammit, Saul, those damn Americans and Russians have screwed up this world so bad, I really wonder if our job is worthwhile." Simon stood there with a disgusted look on his face.

I always got a little nervous when Simon would have one of his temper tantrums. I walked over to the glass door and retrieved the newspaper. The headline read "More U.S.-U.S.S.R. Border Violence Reported."

"But, Simon," I responded in a halfhearted voice, "this situation was inevitable, as you well know. Why do you let it upset you so? You're an American now and have been for a number of years."

"Bullshit," he responded disgustedly. "I'm still a Jew, and our homeland was Israel until those damn Americans camped their fat asses over there."

"Simon, don't be so naïve." I could hear my voice becoming stronger. "You know that this world's lifeline runs on oil, and without it our cars wouldn't run, our homes would be cold, and to be honest, the world would be in a great big frenzy."

"So what! Does that mean every country should bend over backwards and let the Americans and Russians just come walking in and take over?"

"For one thing, Simon," I interrupted, "the Americans and Russians are not in Israel, they are in Saudi Arabia, Iran, and Iraq. They don't affect Israel's domestic or foreign policy in the least; they are just next door to us. Can't you understand that?"

"Saul, as far as I'm concerned, if they're right next to Israel, that's too close for me. Besides, I say they do intervene in the policy of Israel. Why do you think the underground movement is fighting for its freedom?"

Simon walked away, disgusted.

For months Simon had been in a terrible mood. Ever since the takeover of the Middle East, he had been moaning about the subject. I had been angry at first, and could honestly say that I did want to go and aid the resistance, but what could a few patriotic Jews do against two superpowers like the Americans and Russians? The underground movement achieved very little, if anything, except to show both countries that Israel had a history of fighting for what it believed was theirs. Besides, I had never lived in Israel, and America had given me a comfortable life, even though much of my time was spent working.

The situation which had led to the takeover in the Middle East was one of complex variables, and one which had started many years in the past.

The oil problem was a puzzle which most members of the United States government, and the people, never really worried about. Oil pricing had been relatively cheap in the past. In 1960 the cost of a barrel of oil was eighty-two cents. The other two major fossil fuels were natural gas and coal, which were in abundance. Things looked good as far as energy stood for the U.S. back in 1960.

The energy needs of the U.S. changed drastically in the early 1970s. The war was winding down in Vietnam, and also the population of the U.S. was increasing at a much faster rate than anticipated. This also proved to be more than the top-level economic advisers had planned on. The country was going into a recession, plus oil pricing in 1973 was further complicated by an oil embargo. The government realized that it had to find alternate sources of energy and new reserves of oil in order to be more independent of the Organization of Producing and Exporting Countries. This was a band of nations whose main exporting commodity was oil, and in reality, controlled the world price of oil.

The first plan which the government wanted to implement was a get-tough policy. It consisted of threatening the Arab countries with military intervention if they did not lighten up on oil prices.

The second plan was to deny loans to the OPEC nations through the Export-Import Bank, which the U.S. treasury had policy control of. Because of the world situation at the time, the U.S. government decided that developing their own energy sources would be the safest way to achieve an independence from foreign oil, and also to avoid a military confrontation.

England had discovered oil in the North Sea, which would make them virtually independent of foreign oil imports. The price of foreign oil in 1974 was eleven dollars a barrel.

It was time for the U.S. to draft an energy policy that would loosen the Arabs' stranglehold on the country. The name of the policy was "Project Independence." The first order of business was to start a conservation program that would make Americans conscious of the problem at hand. Millions of dollars were spent in an advertising campaign which told people to buy economical cars, turn down their thermostats in the home as much as possible, and to think about how to save energy.

The second solution was to speed completion of the Alaskan Pipeline which would help both industrial and private use as oil consumption rose steadily.

The last three plans consisted of starting strip mining of coal in abundant places, more intense exploration for natural gas reserves, and expanding the construction of more nuclear breeder reactor plants across the country.

The projected oil imports for the year 1985 was nine point seven million barrels a day. This was a previously unheard-of figure.

A few years later the new administration of 1977 adopted a program called "oil stockpiling." The main thrust of this project was to have old salt domes and mines filled with oil. The reason behind this was to take the punch out of an oil price hike, if one should arise without due warning, or if there should be an unforeseen shortage of oil due to an embargo. The major outcome of the U.S. energy policy was that it never really got off the ground.

Major energy legislation was being held up in Congress by the President's not knowing how to play the game with Congress. Most points of the energy package were rejected by Congress and sent back to the President for major reconstruction.

To make the problem even more complex, environmentalists were protesting the government's nuclear power installations under construction in specific places around the U.S. The major problem was how to dispose of nuclear waste materials without endangering people.

While the energy policies of the country struggled to lift off the ground, the situation was constantly getting worse. Inflation was at an all-time high. The President knew that his only alternative was one which he did not want to make, but one that his responsibility for the people was forcing him into.

The takeover in the Middle East had been a shock to the world. Many people were still wondering what had happened, even though various articles had been written in magazines and newspapers around the world.

The invasion of the Middle East had taken place a little over a year ago. It had been planned with the utmost secrecy. The newspapers described the takeover in some detail, but all I can remember was waking up one morning, then picking up the *Times* and unfolding it. The headline read in big bold print "Middle East Countries Invaded by U.S.-U.S.S.R."

For days, almost nothing was on the television but news, keeping people up to date on the joint takeover which affected Iran, Iraq, and Saudi Arabia. The governments of the three countries had been disbanded and martial law was being enforced.

Immediately after stepping down from office, the three leaders made their way by jet to New York in order to speak their opposition to a special meeting of the United Nations. The leaders consisted of Abdel Majid Isam—President of Iraq; Muhsen Ben El Razzak—Muslim leader of Iran; and Moustafah Fatah Allah-sheikh of Saudia Arabia. Their protests were conveyed by many member nations of the world, but other countries did not dare put their protests into action. The fear was annihilation by U.S.-Soviet nuclear weapons, which was a distinct possibility.

At first the American public was up in arms about the whole affair, and was letting its opposition be known to the White House by a flood of mail and protests. Even many American newspapers were condemning the takeover as unnecessary and a slander to the pride of the American people.

The *New York Times*, following the takeover, ran a cartoon in the editorial column. It depicted Soviet Leader Boris Kozloski and President John Sullivan filling up their Cadillacs with gasoline from an oil well in the desert. This was just one of the many cartoons and articles that appeared in newspapers.

In the past year the American economy had changed drastically. The federal budget was well balanced with a reserve amount which stretched into the billion-dollar range. The American people received a tax rebate and federal taxes were also lowered substantially for all classes of people. Cities were receiving millions of dollars to start urban renewal programs to beautify the run-down buildings and parks.

All American oil companies were tightly regulated by the government in how they conducted their business. The oil which they produced had to be sold at a specific price per barrel to the American people and any nation of the world. The price of gasoline had dropped to twenty-five cents per gallon, and this affected the price of automobiles in a drastic reduction of almost forty-nine percent.

It seemed that all industry in the country was prospering from lower oil prices. The American dollar regained its true value, and after a year, the public opinion poll had turned in favor of the government's action toward the Middle East. The American people knew one thing, that their way of life had changed for the better. The lower class was being helped and pushed into the middle class, and crime had decreased greatly. America was virtually a dream world to live in.

The tri-nation borderlines had been set up soon after the takeover and divided the huge oil fields equally. One of the problems which turned out to be quite serious was that the American soldiers and Russian soldiers did not get along with each other, even though they were separated by a border fence. The strain of having to be on the lookout for an underground terrorist attack by the tri-nation community was taking its toll with troops stationed at the border.

The average soldier was in no mood to be diplomatic with a Russian who decided to harass him. Many shooting incidents were reported and looked on with disfavor by both the White House and the Kremlin. The diplomatic leaders of both countries were continuously traveling to meetings in order to explain their country's views on the problems at the border. It was almost as though the Middle East had escalated into an impossible situation.

# Chapter 3

Matto Grasso, Brazil

It was a beautiful, brilliantly clear day, although he knew the intense heat would come later in the afternoon. Bormann and Hans sat on the forward deck, admiring the trees on the river's edge as they made their way slowly upstream. On the way, they passed many of the colony's ranch houses, perched on the river's edge with easy access to escape if some emergency should arise.

They had spent several hours making their way home. The river's edge, flourishing with many colorful flowers, along with masses of jungle greenery, was a lovely spot. They passed a lagoon bordered by a playful school of otters. When the otters came to the surface, they opened their mouths like seals and made a loud hissing sound. Hyacinth macaws screamed harshly as they flew across the river. To their right, capybaras stood perched at the riverbank, staring at them as if dumbfounded.

Bormann slapped his arm just as a mosquito, which had devoured some of his blood, was making its getaway. He was too late. The blood from his body started to dry immediately on his sunbaked arm. Mosquitos were one insect he could never get used to, living in Brazil. It seemed to him that even when you were in midstream, the little insects would haunt you worse than the most persistent Jewish hunter.

He could see the security guards chopping their way through the heavy underbrush further ahead, searching for the slightest hint that any living person was in the area. This signaled them that their journey toward home was almost at an end. That was one good aspect of the security network. All friends of the colony traveled by river, and any enemies would come by land because it would be much harder to detect them in the heavy brush.

As they drew near the rickety little dock, Bormann looked up and viewed the handsome ranch-styled house that stood in a grassy opening, only a few meters from the edge of the river. The surrounding area was dotted with royal palm trees, flower gardens, vegetable gardens, a corral, and two flagpoles—one with the Brazilian flag hoisted, and the other with the Nazi flag.

Hans helped Bormann from the boat to the dock as he had been doing for a long time, realizing that Bormann was not getting any younger. They strolled up the wooden walkway toward the house. Bormann was a little tired from the trip, and also his nerves had been on edge as they always were when leaving his heavily guarded fortress. He knew one of his comrades was more relaxed than others in their security measures, and he did not want to fall into the hands of some hungry Jewish hunters who would probably trade their own mother for a chance to capture him and return him to Israel to stand trial for various war crimes.

They passed two guards at the front door and walked in. Rudolf was standing in the middle of the living room, staring up at a picture of the Fuhrer which was mounted high on the west wall.

"Father," he said with a bewildered look on his face, "you are home earlier than I had anticipated."

"Well," Bormann answered softly, "my business didn't take as long as I had originally planned. Have you been studying hard since I left?"

"Yes, Sir, except for a short walk around the compound."

Rudi walked quickly over to a red velvet loveseat and settled himself down. He was a fine-looking man, forty-three years of age. He was medium height with broad shoulders. His blond hair and high forehead made him look very German, and also very handsome.

"Did you have a pleasant trip down to Herr Baum's villa?" Rudi asked.

"Well Rudi," Bormann said brightly, "Herr Baum is always filled with news of the goings on everywhere. But just between you and me, I'm getting too old for the trip."

"What did Herr Baum have to say, Sir?"

"We discussed the usual things such as security measures, investment statistics, and any world events that might affect us."

Herr Baum was an acquaintance he had meet after they fled to Brazil. He was a loyal Nazi and was versed in economics and the party's views on just about everything. He had been the president of a toy factory in Stuttgart during the war, and ran quite a profitable company, distributing his merchandise all over Europe. When the war was winding down, Baum decided to move with the Nazi party to Brazil because he honestly believed in the party and all it could achieve. He came in very handy corresponding with various men in the area because he was not marked as a Nazi criminal. He could also move freely to many key members' homes without arousing any suspicion.

"Sir," Rudi said, amused, "you can't fool me. I know you visit Herr Baum to drink his imported cognac."

He sat back in the seat with a smug look on his face. Bormann laughed to himself.

"Rudi, you can always see through me and my devious little plans. I'd swear there is a sixth sense in you."

"Well, Sir, I have been advised by one of the great minds of the Third Reich."

"Rudi, Rudi, you are much too kind. If I had had your ability to see the truth and to know what other people were thinking, I could have advised the Fuhrer about many enemies on his staff back in Berlin."

"Father, please don't go over old battlegrounds." Rudi looked a little disgusted, so Bormann left it at that.

Sometimes he thought maybe he had spent too much time babying Rudi and giving him too much attention. Rudolf would obey him much like a little boy, but he was an attentive man, open and willing for new knowledge and information. Bormann felt bad that Rudi was not able to socialize with other people outside the colony, but he was too important to their cause to have him lost in love with a local woman, or a Jewish hunter who might stumble over him accidentally.

His life had been almost a crusade to be the perfect Aryan. The time and energy spent on him was endless. It seemed sometimes that it might not be worth the effort to train the perfect German, but when the right social, economic, and political conditions prevailed, Rudi would be ready to lead the German people. He had had National Socialism drilled into his head until he could preach it in his sleep. He also learned to hate Christianity in all forms, whether it was Catholic or Protestant or any belief. Rudi shared the most radical Nazi ideology, whether about the evil of the Jews and Slavs, or the duty of the German woman to reproduce in or out of wedlock. Bormann spoke to him about the mixture of blood in the German state, and how it could only be corrected if the lowest elements were weeded out.

He was taught stringently about the writings in *Mein Kamph*. This was regarded as the bible of National Socialism. The seven points of the business of the state were drilled into Rudi's head. They were as follows:

The race must be the center of attention.

The race must be kept clean.

Birth control must be practiced by all non-Germans, and all diseased, weak people should not be able to reproduce.

The state must promote sports among young people.

The state must make the army the final and highest school.

The state must emphasize the teaching of racial knowledge in the schools.

The state must awaken patriotism and national pride among citizens.

Bormann always made Rudi read books of history to show him these valid points. Also, economic theories were expressed at great length by Rudi's teachers. They showed him that national self-sufficiency and economic independence had to replace international trade. They had to break off from this if they wanted to stop it.

A main point which was also taught was that of international finance and loan capitalism. This had to be destroyed in order to free the people from this interest slavery. It was important that the banking system was put in governmental control. Money for all public works projects, such as water, power, and roads, had to be obtained through government coupons which bore no interest.

One of the most important things which Rudi was trained in was his oratory. Bormann assisted him and also used many specialized tutors who were schooled in speaking. Rudi acquired a special way of picking up a speech and belting it out so loud and forcefully that you would utterly believe every word it contained.

Bormann was very proud of Rudi, and of the things he had taught him throughout his life. He believed that Rudi would be ready for duty when the time was right.

Their preparations had started even before the end of the War. Bormann remembered back on Christmas Day, 1944, when a variety of senior war officials had received unexpected presents. They consisted of false identification papers, passports, birth certificates, and work permits. This was done by a special unit of the Gestapo. These documents would assist the men to flee the country if the end of the Reich was near. Along with these preparations, an organization was set up to help the escape of Nazi personnel from Germany. Its name was Die Schleuse (Lock Gates.) The Gestapo's head man, Heinrich Mueller, and his men began compiling lists and guides of people who lived near the frontiers of Switzerland and Italy. In Schleswig-Holstein they recruited men who knew all the smugglers' routes into Denmark. Most people whom the Gestapo contacted to help were ones who had collaborated with them at one time or another. They had the choice of helping or being denounced to the Allies as traitors.

One escape route led north through the towns of Kiel, Schleswig, and Flensburg into Denmark. A number of Nazis then escaped from there via plane to Argentina with the help of General Peron, Dictator of the country. Many top German scientists and technicians were the first to leave in order to avoid capture by the Allies.

The southern escape route was far more important. Most routes led to Munich and then split up. They could cross the frontier at Kufstein or Scharnitz, or go southwest through Memminger, reach the shores of Lake Constance at Lindau, and then follow it around into Switzerland. From there they could continue either into France or Italy.

Most Lock Gates agents were local people, so they were familiar with the surrounding area. Once into France or Italy, the agent would secretly transport them to the coast and smuggle them aboard a ship bound for either Spain, the Middle East, or South America.

Even after the war, many other such organizations were set up to assist the movement of Bormann's comrades. One such group was Die Spinne, or the Spider. It began in the autumn of 1948 in a prisoner of war camp at Glasenbach. The main function of this group was to distribute and receive Nazi doctrines on National Socialism. They also had escape routes and organized members to smuggle wanted men out of the country.

Another related group was the HIAG. It was set up in 1951 and its members were men who served in the Waffen SS. Those affiliated with the group collected money to help little German orphans. Little did they know that the money went to help strengthen escape and propaganda organizations.

The last important organization was the Odessa. It was very closely knit with the Spider and provided well for its members with funds from German businessmen. Most of the German youth movements were financed by this. Its local contacts served to help a captured comrade get a lawyer, put some pressure on judges, or do away with inconvenient witnesses.

Even though organizations to help their people escape and to go underground were important, their economic rebuilding was much more significant in order to achieve the final means to survive in a world that, for the most part, hated Nazis and would never forget the so-called atrocities.

Their economic program was one of extensive detail. Members of the Party, German industrialists, and army leaders, realizing that victory was lost, prepared plans for the postwar period. Some of their people renewed connections with industrial leaders in order to re-establish prewar cartels. Many Nazi chiefs had prepared for the future, too. They had deposited large sums of money with banks in neutral countries, and put millions into portfolios of apparently respectable persons in Liechtenstein, Portugal, and Patagonia. Some additional money had also been hidden deep in old salt mines in Austria, or below the dark waters of the Alpine lakes. These funds, however, did not constitute the majority of the Reich's wealth in Latin America.

In 1944, Bormann gave orders to put the Land of Fire Operation into full force. This operation involved the transport from Germany to Argentina of several tons of gold, securities, and some priceless works of art.

Some of the gold was taken from the teeth of corpses dragged from the gas chambers of Auschwitz and Treblinka. Most of the precious artwork and statues had been taken from many European museums and sent to Berlin. Truck convoys sped through Germany and France to Spanish ports where U-boats were waiting to receive the precious cargo.

The smuggling of Nazis to a new home would have never been possible without a friendly atmosphere. As far back as 1933, when the Nazi party came to power, the Nazis were making a special effort to spread their doctrine throughout South American countries. Many German colonies were already strongly established in many parts of Latin America.

One of the most popular colonies was in Brazil, at Blumenau and Florianopolis, in the federal state of Santa Catarina. Everything was, and still is, very reminiscent of Germany, such as the countryside, the style of houses, the appearance of the people, and their speech. It was also the same in many regions of Argentina. In Paraguay, many thousands of German immigrants had cleared and cultivated areas to the east of Asuncion, and had given their towns names like Hohenau, to remind them of their origins.

Strangely enough, most of this immigration to South America had taken place in order to escape the rule of Kaiser Wilhelm II.

The generation of Germans born in their new home were brought up in a tight little Nazi world. They were inevitably attracted by the dynamic doctrines of National Socialism. The presence of the Nazi people greatly facilitated the spread of Nazi movements in Latin American countries. Many people enjoyed and admired their presence because they believed that Germans were very efficient, disciplined, and had great organizing ability. This was one virtue their own people lacked. Thus Bormann, and other leaders of the Third Reich, found loyal and faithful allies. In addition, the Nazi people were already strongly entrenched in these countries and held important jobs in the economic, social, and political fields.

In 1955, after Juan Peron's fall from power, many high-ranking Nazi comrades left for other South American countries, or Spain, the Middle East, and even the United States. Peron had offered a friendly atmosphere for the Nazi people, and many were not optimistic as to the relationship they would have with the new Aramburu government. Many decided to retreat into the interior and make their homes in the arid uplands, the empty pampas, or the jungle, far from civilization.

The wide pampas, stretching away from the Parana River where the frontier of Argentina meets that of Paraguay and Brazil, became a preserve for high-ranking Nazis who were constantly under the threat of capture by Jewish hunters—most of whom did not forget the deaths of their families and others during World War II.

The Matto Grasso proved to be the ideal spot for this preserve of German officials. The huge unexplored tropical jungle, with its swamps, was barely navigable except for a few rivers and two rough roads. The approach of any stranger from the outside world would be known several days in advance. Originally, the Matto Grasso had been a place of refuge for mobs of fugitives, escaped convicts, and wanted criminals. Bormann's home was the best possible place to live as long as present conditions prevailed.

Bormann sat down in his favorite brown leather chair to relax.

"Hans," he said weakly, "could you get me my smoking jacket and slippers? I would like to sit here for a bit and read for a while before I retire to my room."

Hans turned quickly from thumbing through a magazine.

"Herr Reichsleiter, would you like me to mix a drink to soothe your aching bones?"

"No, Hans, just bring me my jacket and slippers...then you are dismissed for the rest of the day."

"As you wish, Sir," he replied. Hans left the room very promptly. He was the only person Bormann knew who could work hard all day long and never tire. He was always doing things to please Bormann. It reminded him of the days around the Reich Chancellery. At that time, Bormann was also constantly running around, trying to anticipate the Fuhrer's next order. It gave Bormann great pleasure to serve him in all capacities.

Still deep in thought, he looked up at his picture high on the wall and wondered if their colony would ever get the chance to take up where the Third Reich left off. All he could do was hope and plan, if the day should ever come.

Bormann suddenly awoke from a day dream standing in the middle of the living room. In the dining area he heard voices, so he glanced across the hallway. Rudi had enticed Hans into a game of chess, which inevitably Hans would lose. That crazy old fool would never give up trying, either. Bormann was weary from the day's journey and retired to his bedroom.

## Chapter 4

Warren, Vermont 6 January 1984

The chairlift was moving right along as we approached the summit unloading station. A chilly breeze cut through me, tickling the bottom of my spine and sending shivers to my neck. I took my ski mitten off one hand and pushed back the sleeve of my parka to look at my watch. It read a quarter to four. This should be the last run of the afternoon, I thought.

The day had been a good one in which I was able to make several runs, it being a weekday and the ski crowd being relatively thin. I always loved this time of year, when Simon and I could get away and relax for a while.

It was too bad Itka had not been able to join us this year, but her mounting responsibilities as a physician had confined her to the hospital. Simon was very disappointed in her decision to stay home, even though I assured him he would more than likely run into some female companionship to drown his sorrows.

The chairlift bumped its way over the last hard, black rollers on the way to the unloading ramp. I opened my safety bar and put the tips of my skis up in the air. I stood up out of my chair and breezed down the ramp, then took a quick right toward my favorite trail. As I was gliding down the small grade, I took one last look across the

Green Mountains. The sun was getting close to the top of a mountain west of my location. The air was clean and the sky was so clear, I could see for many miles in any direction.

My speed had increased considerably in just a few second's time. The trees on both sides of the trail were whistling by me. It was time for a couple of fast turns to level off my speed.

The hill was virtually deserted except for some lingering ski patrol personnel and a few hotshots taking their last runs. The air seemed to be getting very brisk the further I went down the hill and I thought how much difference the sun made in keeping a person somewhat warm while he was skiing.

My speed was just about right as I weaved my way down the shaded mountain. My ski hit a big bump and I took an unexpected glide through the air. The moguls were so shadowed that the hill appeared perfectly smooth all the way down to the base lodge. My leg muscles began to ache quite a bit, not being used to skiing for so long down the mountain, but I was determined to do it in one try.

The lights of the base lodge were beaming brighter the closer I came. I decided to really fly the last leg of the hill in case Simon was watching from the base lodge. If by chance he was there with some female company, you could be guaranteed he would have built me up as big as Jean Claude Kiley.

My speed was increasing rapidly and my turns became short and tight. My body was crouched low and my hips were rotating with ease. The wind was becoming colder as I boomed down the white clustered slope. My eyes began to tear the faster I went. This had to be one of the greatest feelings on earth, to come down a hill with such speed and gracefulness. My mind was at complete ease.

The finishing stop created a whirlwind of spraying powder. The light from the lodge created prisms in the snow as it came fluttering back down to earth. I released out of my skis and ran quickly into the lodge.

People were buzzing around the immediate area—mothers retrieving their children, people getting something to eat, and friends talking over the day's activities. I made my way to the stairs and stomped down them into the lounge.

The crowd on hand was a good-sized one, consisting of many different age groups. I proceeded to scan the crowd for Simon and spotted him next to the windows, opposite the bar. Sure enough, he was entertaining two young ladies and my luck was running well, too—there was a chair saved for me.

I sidestepped my way through the crowd, being cautious not to bump anyone's drink. Simon had spotted me and started waving his arm enthusiastically. I stepped up to the table and stared down at the two young ladies.

"Saul," Simon spoke politely, "I would like you to meet Nancy and Jane. They're secretaries at a big law firm in Boston."

"Pleased to meet you," I responded in a meek voice, which I wished I could have retrieved. I cleared my throat and continued. "So you girls are secretaries. Are you mixed up in any paralegal work at all?"

They looked at each other and giggled. Then Nancy spoke up.

"You're so right, Saul. We have been doing paralegal for about two years."

"Is it interesting?" I responded with a growing authority in my voice.

She agreed, nodding her head and with a great big smile on her face. Simon waved the waitress over and ordered a round of drinks. I had my usual—vodka and tonic with a lime. The first sip tasted great sliding down my parched throat and seemed to bring me back to life. I looked over at Simon; he was giving me some sort of stupid high sign with his eyes and forehead. He appeared to be hinting that Nancy was mine.

Well, that was fine with me. Nancy was an attractive girl of about twenty-eight years, with beautiful, long black hair. Her eyes were a brilliant blue, and her skin was very soft looking, with a cute turned-up nose. She was wearing red and white bib ski pants with a red sweater to match.

"Saul," Nancy darted out, "Simon won't tell us what you both do for a living. Why can't we know?"

I looked at Simon right away and he started laughing jubilantly.

"Well, girls," Simon chuckled, "we are really CIA agents sent here to spy on pretty little secretaries from Boston."

Jane grabbed Simon's ski hat and pulled it down over his eyes. I could still hear him slyly snickering behind the hat.

"Well, girls," I said, "Simon tends to tell tales out of school. Our real profession is consulting various international corporations on marketing procedures. We travel to several cities whenever our services are needed."

Jane jumped right in the conversation.

"You mean you fly all over the world and companies pay you to do it?"

"Well, yes," I replied, "many corporations all over the world need our advice. Say, for instance, a company has a new product, but it just hasn't had the right approach to get it to sell on the retail market. The company in turn brings us in and we advise them how to turn the advertising campaign around."

"And you mean this gets the product to sell successfully?" Jane replied in a questioning voice.

"Sure. Ninety nine percent of the time it does."

Simon sat back in his chair, putting his hands on the back of his head. The look on his face was one of sheer content.

"Now, girls," Simon gurgled out, "I have a great idea."

The girls turned to look at Simon.

"How about if I grab this waitress and order us another round of drinks?"

They nodded in agreement.

"And I'll tell you what," he continued, "I won't even charge you two for my great idea."

I looked over at Nancy and glanced into her eyes to catch her reaction. All of a sudden she burst out laughing, followed by Jane and myself. Simon sat weaving back and forth in his chair, clutching Jane's arm and patting the top of her hand like a damn fool. But what the hell, he was a pretty funny guy when he wanted to be.

While our conversation was flowing right along, I could hear a folk guitar playing rhythmically in the background. My curiosity finally got the best of me. I looked away from Nancy and focused in on the tiny stage perched over by the corner of the room, near the windows at the other end. There stood a rather small man with light skin and a sort of sugar bowl haircut—rather like one of the Beatles in the sixties. He was strumming a six-string folk guitar with some sort of microphone hookup to make the guitar sound louder while he was playing. He was going on about how he was educated at the Berkley School of Music in Boston.

I had always loved music, but never had the time nor money to get mixed up in it seriously. That's probably why I appreciated good music so much.

The guitarist proceeded into a peppy version of some folk song and both Nancy and Jane joined in singing with the rest of the crowd. I looked across to Simon. He was mouthing something to me. I really couldn't understand him because he had a ferocious case of the hiccups. He kicked me gently under the table and started mouthing the word 'food' to me. I acknowledged that I understood him and continued sipping my drink. My stomach seemed to feel very empty once I started thinking about food.

As the music died down, I asked Nancy and Jane to join us for a bite to eat back at our condominium. They both seemed very pleased to join us, so we finished our drinks and left.

********

My eyes peeked open to the sound of a telephone ringing loudly. I struggled to my bedside table to answer the ungodly noise. My head was pounding to the sound of my heart. What in God's name did I do last night?

I lifted the receiver to my mouth. "Hello," I said softly.

"Saul! Saul! Is that you?" a harsh voice asked.

I thought to myself for a moment. Who was this desperate sounding man?

"Herman?" I whispered inquisitively.

"Yes, Saul. Thank God I've finally reached you. I've been so scared and afraid."

"What happened, Herman? What are you afraid of?"

"The Nazis" he blurted out. "I think they've killed Sidney," he said, gasping for a breath of air.

My heart began pounding like a kettle drum.

"You were supposed to stay with him at all times. This rule was not to be broken. Why did you do such a thing?" I could hear myself becoming very loud and brassy.

Herman Kreisberg and Sidney Rubenstein had been two of our closest friends and business partners. For many years, they had had a very good reason to be hunting Nazi war criminals. Both Herman's and Sidney's parents had died in the gas chambers of Auschwitz in 1942, and they both had spent the rest of the war in a labor camp somewhere in Germany. They were two of the lucky ones who had escaped the gas chamber. After the war, both of them moved to Israel and worked in a documentation center in Haifa. After a few years they decided that more productive work could be done in the field.

The men had met Simon and I by coincidence in an airport lounge in Sao Paulo. Herman accidentally spilled his drink on Simon at the bar. After a near battle broke out, Sidney and I calmed the two down. I settled the skirmish by buying a round of drinks. After some conversation, our mutual occupations came out, so we decided to swap information and work together.

Their general plan throughout the years was to travel around in potential areas where rumors were heard, and to pick up any helpful information from the residents.

The last time we had seen the two was in New York City about a month ago. Simon decided to take Sidney out for his birthday since he would be leaving on a trip to Asuncion, Paraguay, for quite some time.

"I'm sorry, Saul," Herman pleaded, "I couldn't help it. It was all Sidney's idea. He just had to find out for himself."

"Settle down, Herman, settle down," I consoled him. "Exactly what went on?"

"Well, one night we strolled into an old bar in Asuncion, just running down some flimsy leads. We started up a conversation with a man who said he was an Austrian born doctor who had lived in Germany. At the end of the war, he decided to come to Paraguay to reside. After we heard this, Sidney kept buying the man drink after drink, hoping to get him to give us some helpful information on German citizens in the area."

There was a silence for a moment.

"Herman! Are you there, Herman?"

"Yes, I'm all right, Saul, but listen. This guy was really getting drunk, right? Well, he started mumbling something about Martin Bormann."

"What?!" I gasped.

I could hardly believe my ears. My adrenalin was flowing at an extremely high rate. It was as if an alarm had gone off in my body. Martin Bormann, the second most powerful person in the Third Reich. I couldn't believe I was hearing someone mention his name.

Simon and I had been searching for this man ever since the Eichmann capture in 1961, in vain. We probably knew more about Martin Bormann than we knew about our own parents.

Martin Bormann was a true phantom, who was never proven dead or alive by any concrete evidence. His face popped up in more than a dozen countries around the world, but no one was able to verify it positively. His face was not known to the masses of people like Hitler's, because he never really liked to get his picture taken and was rarely seen by the public.

There were many theories about Bormann's whereabouts and his death. After the Reichsleiter emerged from the Bunker on that May evening in 1945, the fighting was wild and furious. Many persons believed that he made his escape as far as the bridge over the Invalidenstrasse, where Dr. Ludwig Stumpfegger and he ran into a Russian-German crossfire. Arthur Axmann, the leader of Hitler's Youth Movement, verified this to German authorities after the war. Somehow the Russians did not recognize him, and tossed his body into an unmarked mass grave. Axmann said he picked up a diary containing Bormann's name while scurrying by, but somehow had lost it.

Many other stories arose from intense investigations after the fighting had ceased. The Central Intelligence Agency in 1953 came up with a few interesting theories of their own.

The first was one which made Bormann look like a traitor to the Soviet Union. He was supposedly a top informer who was to go as instructed to the Invalidenstrasse where his death was faked. After this, he was smuggled out of Berlin back to Russia where he advised the Russians on German affairs and lived in harmony.

A second and similar theory was one which had Bormann as a British Intelligence Agent. Rudolf Hess, who had flown to Scotland, was in association with Bormann. When Hess's mission failed, Bormann was put in contact with the Englanders. This was backed up by his determination to reach Admiral Doenitz. His real mission was to go toward Plon, France, where he would be taken by British Forces and returned to England.

The third and final theory was very believable, and was the story that all Jewish hunters lived by. They surmised that if Bormann had really thought the situation was hopeless, he would have committed suicide with Hitler and Goebbels at the Bunker.

Most of the stories told after the war were to confuse the investigation or to dull it to a point. Simon and I had developed a theory that Bormann reached the Baltic coast, where he escaped by German U-boat to Argentina. There he was protected by the Fascist Dictator Peron and lived on millions of marks taken from the Nazi treasury. His guards were former SS men, and his life was carried on with top Nazi party officials.

The ending to the theory was enough to scare Simon and Saul into devoting their full attention to Martin Bormann. The secretary was believed to be directing a worldwide Nazi conspiracy with the final goal of establishing a fourth Reich with Bormann as its leader.

At the Eichmann trial, a startling event occurred. A postcard arrived, along with many other letters, having to do with the Eichmann proceedings. It contained three words: "Mut, Mut, Martin." This meant courage, courage, Martin. When Eichmann was questioned about the subject, he admitted that Bormann was alive and well.

In 1973, city workers in Berlin dug up what was identified as the remains of SS Colonel Ludwig Stumpfegger, near the Lehrte Railway Station. Beside him was a smaller man who was presumed to be Martin Bormann.

Later, in 1974, a leading author said he had a meeting with Bormann at a nursing home in Bolivia. The author was supposedly informed by Bormann that he had escaped from Europe aided by a Vatican passport. After the interview, Bormann was returned to

Buenos Aires where he lived in a lavish home and had a neo-Nazi regime.

********

I heard a faint voice blurting my name "Saul, Saul, are you there?" The voice sounded very nervous.

"I'm sorry, Herman. Are you sure he —" Herman cut me off midway through.

"Saul, I'm positive. Listen ... he said a girl came to his house one night saying a man was very ill and needed his help. The man traveled with her for hours into a remote jungle in Brazil. They arrived at a ranch house and were hustled in by several guards. There he treated a man for a bleeding duodenal ulcer."

"Well, how did he know it was Bormann?" I interrupted.

Herman continued.

"He said he knew exactly what Bormann looked like from photographs he had seen in books and in newspapers. After he finished treating him, the girl took him back to Asuncion and warned him not to speak a word, or it could mean his life." Herman paused, then continued. "Well, anyway, he spilled his guts to us. He even told us Bormann's whereabouts. It was supposed to be about twenty-four kilometers north of Paraguay, on the western bank of the Parana River."

My heart continued to pump rapidly, and the palms of my hands were so sweaty that I had to regrip the telephone receiver. I couldn't believe what I was hearing. Herman's voice was speeding up with nervous anxiety mixed in.

"Slow down, Herman. Take your time ... tell it right," I advised.

"I'm so scared and mixed up, Saul. Sidney's dead." He began to whimper.

"Don't worry, Herman ... it's not your fault. You know Sidney always had to do things his way."

The crying ceased after a moment.

"Uh, uh ...where was I? Oh, then Sidney got it in his head to follow the doctor's directions and verify his information. So we went back to the rooming house and he grabbed his two-way radio, the special microphone bug, and some rations for a few days. I begged him not to go alone, but he insisted that if he got caught, he wanted the world to know where this murderer was living."

"Go on, Herman, what else happened?" I was becoming very anxious for the inescapable truth.

"I was waiting in my room with the two-way radio set on. The time seemed to pass slowly, and I was so apprehensive that I almost called him to check and see if he was all right. After a couple of days, he contacted me. His voice was filled with joyous fear."

"How did he get there? Did he have any help?"

"No, no," Herman said in a disgusted sort of way. "Wait till you hear this. He had made his way right up to the point where the jungle met the back grounds of Bormann's villa. As he scanned the yard to see where the guards were posted, he noticed two liquor glasses half full on a patio table. He decided to throw his bugging device over by the table so he could eavesdrop on whoever was sitting there. After a few minutes, two older men came from the house and sat at the table. Sidney said it was Bormann with no doubt in his mind. His hair had grayed and his receding hairline had turned into a balding head, but he was sure. The other man wasn't known to Sidney at all. His bugging device was not coming in very well, but good enough to hear."

I moved and sat on the floor by the bed, trying to avoid the sun which was just rising over the mountains and pitching a harsh ray of light in my eyes, and listened in anticipation to the gruesome facts.

Herman continued in a tired, depressed voice.

"Saul, this story is so bizarre, I don't know how it could possibly be true. Well, the two men started talking. The only thing Sidney could figure out from the conversation was something about a man named Kaminski who was really a Nazi agent and scientist but had defected to the Russians at the end of the war. He must have worked his way up in the Russian defense command because he apparently has access to the nuclear defensive and offensive weapons control centers."

I jumped up as if I was shot out of a cannon. "Are you sure, Herman? Couldn't Sidney have read this thing all wrong?"

"No," Hermann replied in a disgusted voice.

"Is this Kaminski fellow going to send off a nuclear bomb?"

"No, he is going to fake a nuclear missile being shot at the United States."

"What will this accomplish?"

Sidney continued.

"Most of the United States' nuclear offensive missiles are programmed at certain targets in the Soviet Union, so if they think they are being attacked by them, they will send these missiles off before the Soviet ones destroy their launching pads and bases."

"Would the United States really believe they were being attacked?" I questioned.

"Sure!" Herman insisted. "With the growing tensions in the Middle East, the Americans would believe that in a moment. Whoever came out on top after the war would control the oil fields and have enough oil for three hundred years."

I bowed my head and thought for a second.

"Did Sidney mention when it might happen?"

"That's what is so awful about it all. As he was talking to me, he suddenly stopped in the middle of a sentence. I heard a voice in the background saying *Don't move!* Then the radio quit on me as if it had been smashed. The only thing I can figure out is that it sounded like it would happen soon."

"When did all this happen?"

"Just a few hours ago," Herman replied.

I thought for a moment. What were we going to do?

"Herman, you catch the next plane leaving Asuncion for New York. Simon and I will meet you at his apartment as soon as possible. Tell Itka what happened and wait there."

Herman interrupted.

"I already spoke with Itka. That's how I got your number."

"That's right. I'll see you there, and hurry."

The phone clicked in my ear. I ran out of my room to wake up Simon. What were we going to do? This was completely beyond my comprehension. If we called the Defense Department, they would surely think we were crazy. There was no way of stopping what was going to happen.

I woke Simon and Jane out of a sound sleep and relayed the story to Simon in the bathroom. He was in a state of rage over Sidney's whereabouts and the unbelievable story which accompanied the news.

We stood there thinking and watching the cigarette smoke swirling around the room as the sun's rays magnified its path.

We finally decided to tell Jane what was going on, except for the story about the nuclear espionage. She listened intently with a look of amazement at our tales of woe. All three of us sat on a red sleeper couch, staring out toward the snow-glistened mountain and wondering what to do next.

A loud rap on the front door broke the silence. I glanced out the window and noticed a green sedan parked outside with a United States Government emblem on the driver's door. Three men were sitting in the car wearing what looked like army uniforms. I walked swiftly over to the door and opened it. There stood a tall man, dressed in a green army uniform and displaying a very stern look on his face.

"Can I help you, Sir?" I said in a nervous voice.

"Yes, you can," the man responded quickly. "The management of the ski area would like you to report to the main lounge for a meeting with them as soon as possible."

"Can I ask what this is all about?" I questioned.

"Sir, I'm not at liberty to divulge that information to you. I must stress, though, that it is very important that you report over to the lounge as soon as possible. Good day, Sir."

The man turned and walked back to the car. I glanced over at Simon and Jane.

"What do you suppose that was all about?" I asked.

"I have no idea," Jane answered.

I moved my eyes over to meet Simon's. From his expression, I could see the look of doom across his face. Perspiration was starting to form on my brow. Was it already happening? I would not let myself jump to conclusions until I heard some facts. Maybe it was something completely off the subject. Only time would tell the truth.

********

The volume of noise inside the lounge was extremely loud from the people wondering why they had been summoned to this gathering. Many parties of people were scurrying about, gathering chairs for their family and friends to be comfortable. Simon, Jane, and I had perched ourselves at the bar. Simon sat there, nervously swiveling himself back and forth on his bar stool. Jane sat next to him with a cool, calm look across her face unknowing of the possible news to come.

I glanced over at the doorway and noticed five uniformed men standing there discussing something with their superior officer. From the officer's uniform and badges, he looked like a colonel. He was carrying a bunch of maps under his arm. One of the other men carried a stack of newspapers. The men made their way up front by the plate glass windows and began setting up an easel. The other men were perched by both exits leaving the lounge. They were carrying what looked like M16 rifles.

The colonel began tapping his map pointer on the table in front of him. He then started shouting.

"Attention, attention ...could we please come to order here."

The conversation diminished to silence.

"I suppose you people would like to know why you've all been summoned here," he said in a thunderous voice.

A slight murmur came from the crowd.

"Well, the situation as it stands now, is that the United States, at twenty-two hundred hours yesterday, sustained its first nuclear attack from the Russians."

The crowd broke out in a roar of voices and questions. The colonel began smashing his pointer on the table to restore order in the room. Jane buried her face in Simon's shoulder and began to cry. Simon tried to comfort her, but it was no use. The colonel continued as the noise level diminished.

"People ... people ... please calm yourselves. The worst possible event that could follow this tragedy is mass panic."

A map of the country had been put up behind the colonel. It was very colorful, with red marks on every major city and some other spots which I took to be military installations. The colonel continued.

"The attack was one of immense proportion, but our country will survive this."

A lady jumped out of her chair and shouted, "What does the red mark on New York City mean?"

"The red marks stand for direct hits by a nuclear device."

"What does that mean?" the lady responded harshly.

"This means that New York City and all cities on this map have been completely annihilated."

The noise level rose to a roaring mixture of people crying and questions being thrown at the colonel.

I looked over to my left and spotted Nancy making her way toward me. She threw herself into my arms. I could hear her crying softly.

"It's all right, Nancy, everything will be all right."

I tried to comfort her as best I could. She lifted her head slowly, her face red with tears flowing down her cheeks.

"Saul," she said erratically, "my family and friends ...they're all dead."

All I could do was to comfort her. The only alternative was to sit and listen to the colonel for instructions on what to do. A private was making his way through the crowd, handing out copies of a local Montreal newspaper. The headline read in big bold print, "United States Attacked by Russians." I began to read down the columns of print. It reviewed what cities had been completely destroyed. From what I read in the article, New York City was now an eight-hundred-foot-deep hole in the ground. It had sustained a direct hit by a nuclear device fired from a Soviet submarine. The device, called a Sark-Serb, was a Russian intermediate range ballistic missile containing a hundred megaton warhead. The article explained that the population really had no chance to react to the bomb at all. The explosion carried some fifty thousand feet up into the stratosphere with a temperature of two hundred million degrees. Everything within thirteen miles of the penetration point was completely devastated. When a bomb with such intensity is dropped, people who were fifty to seventy miles away would sustain second degree burns on all exposed skin and wooden houses would explode into flames. Only the lucky people who were more than one hundred and fifty miles away from any blast had a chance of living. As the article continued, it went on to say that the Soviet Union had also been devastated by a series of U.S. made nuclear missiles, which were called Minutemen III and contained a multiple, independent reentry vehicle that were capable of sending a single missile up at a target; then several missiles would be fired from the one warhead toward other targets in Russia. The outcome was devastating. Most of the populated areas of Russia were now barren wasteland. Much of the fallout from these explosions had been carried by winds into China. The situation was just about the same there as it was in the U.S. People who had survived the nuclear blast were dying like flies from radiation sickness.

Other countries that had been directly attacked were England, France, Germany, Japan, Turkey, parts of the Philippines, and several other areas hit by misguided nuclear missiles.

The situation back in the U.S. was hopeless. The predictions from top U.S. officials were that fourteen days from now, about ninety percent of the country's population would be either dead from the attack or from radiation sickness.

The article went on to say that a human's tolerance to radiation was under seven hundred roentgens, which was a dosage measure of radiation. Many people in coastal areas had been killed by tidal waves from aftershocks of nuclear missiles that had exploded in the ocean. A tidal wave contained some hundred thousand roentgens of killing power.

Regarding the defensive missiles, they could not handle the immense volume of missiles fired on the U.S. The Anti-Ballistic Missile fired from Nike bases around the U.S. only contained some thirty percent of the attack power thrown at the U.S. mainland. The cities were virtually helpless, since most of the defensive missiles were used to guard the offensive missiles and their launching pads.

The colonel continued answering questions. One man raised his hand.

"Is the President dead?" the man questioned.

"Yes, Sir, I'm afraid the President and many top-level officials weren't able to escape in time." The colonel bowed his head in despair. The room was one of remorse and fear. "Our Poseidon submarines and all remaining ships and planes have been summoned to Europe and the Middle East to retrieve all U.S. troops to guard the country and its direct borders."

A man sitting next to Simon stepped off his stool and shouted, "Exactly who the hell is left alive in this country?"

"Well, Sir," the colonel cleared his throat, "the people who were up-wind from any nuclear blast will probably survive the fallout. The people who I'm sure are still alive are the military personnel at the North American Air Defense Command in Colorado Springs, and several such bases scattered around the U.S. They are several hundred feet underground and could sustain a direct hit by a nuclear missile without damage to anything or anybody."

"What about the civilian population?" the man shouted. "Who the hell protected them?"

The crowd began to join in agreement. The atmosphere quickly became very hostile.

The colonel began smashing his pointer harder and harder to bring the crowd to order. All of a sudden, the angered man began pushing his way through people to get at the colonel. Two privates stationed at the corners of the room scurried to the colonel to protect him. The man was screaming, "I'll get you, you bastard!"

He finally reached the colonel and grabbed him by the shoulder. The colonel raised his arms to defend himself. The two men jawed at each other while the people stood by and watched.

At that moment, one of the privates leaped over a civilian and hit the man in the face with his rifle. The man immediately fell to the floor in pain. He was semiconscious and mumbling something. It sounded as though he was saying, "Margaret, please be alive, Margaret." He repeated it over and over.

The colonel stood up and tried to regain his composure while two privates attended to the man on the floor.

"People, please take your seats. Please, let's not panic. Things are under control." The colonel was visibly shaken by the episode, but he continued. "The best advice I can give to you at this time is to stay here at the ski area and do not, I repeat, do not try to make your way home. These populated areas will not be safe to go to for at least two months. The country is now under martial law until further notice. Your present housing will continue to be at your disposal and food will be flown in at the earliest possible time. Please go home to your shelters and remain calm. Try to comfort your loved ones."

The crowd began to split up and file out the exits, muttering over what they had just heard. I glanced over at Simon and saw him with his head bowed. Tears streamed from his eyes like a leaky faucet. I knew, and he knew, that Itka was dead. There was no possible way she could have gotten out alive. The whimpering was beginning to drift into silence as the last of the people made their way out the doors.

A sick feeling began gurgling in my stomach. The information from Herman had been true. Somehow Martin Bormann and several other men had started this horrible episode. But why? What could he and his cohorts possibly gain from having the U.S. and the Russians annihilate themselves? The question weighed heavily on my mind as I tried to comfort Nancy.

## Chapter 5

Berlin, Germany   18 April 1985

The view from the television tower's Telecafe Lounge was simply breathtaking. The lounge, located some two hundred meters above the ground, overlooked the Alexanderplatz and gave a fantastic view of the greater Berlin area. As Bormann gazed across the city, he observed the many changes that had taken place since his departure in 1945. Much of the city had been rebuilt after the end of the war, since most of Berlin had been in ruins from the endless and brutal bombing raids delivered by the Allied Forces. From his seat, Bormann could see the Brandenburg Gate and the newly reconstructed Reichstag where the German Parliament was housed. He remembered back to 1933, when those fanatical Bolsheviks burned the Reichstag down.

"How could they have been such stupid fools?" he wondered.

The fire had produced exactly the result the Nazis had anticipated: the Weimar Constitution went up in flames and the Third Reich rose triumphantly from this episode. Berlin itself had been divided by the Berlin Wall since August of 1961. The two different sectors were so dissimilar, it was like night and day. The western sector resembled a bustling metropolis, much like Sao Paulo, Brazil, with its traffic, a variety of hotels, and neon lighting. It had a modern air to it which gave it an inspiring outlook.

The eastern sector was something quite different. It resembled the days when Bormann had been in Berlin. The gray cobblestone streets and the housing appeared very much the same. Automobiles were one of the scarcer articles, with most people walking, riding bicycles, or taking public transportation to reach their destinations.

As he gazed down below, he noticed the bulldozers still dismantling the Berlin Wall near Friedrichstrasse and Zimmerstrasse. This had been better known then as Check Point Charlie. It was one of the main places where people had to pass through in order to move from the communist portion of Berlin to the western portion and was controlled by NATO Forces and West German soldiers.

The wall itself was roughly forty-eight kilometers long between East and West Berlin, with its border around Western Berlin measuring one hundred and sixty kilometers. The main wall, which stretched close to fourteen hundred and thirty kilometers, and ran from the Baltic to Czechoslovakia, contained some two thousand watchtowers and had been guarded by fifty thousand soldiers during one period of the war.

Russian political figures holding office at the time the wall was built said it was an inevitable situation since the western sector offered a better life to the population of Germans. Every morning the East Germans would awaken to find another merchant gone to the West. Many doctors, lawyers, school teachers, and qualified engineers had left, to the Communist's disenchantment. The workforce was being drained, with roughly half of the people being younger than twenty-five years of age. At that time, the East Germans looked at the wall as a permanent solution to the East's deteriorating economic situation.

As Bormann gazed back toward the bar, he noticed a man walking toward his table. He was a good-looking man of average height, with blue eyes and a very profound receding hairline. He walked with a slight limp. He wore a smart-looking, vested tweed suit with a blue tie.

The man approached the table and slipped into the seat facing Bormann.

"Wagner, how have you been?" he said sternly.

"Very well, Herr Stolz," Bormann responded in a low voice.

"I'm glad you remembered my name. People these days don't always remember a man's name, especially in these fast-paced times."

Herr Stolz had not forgotten to call Martin Bormann by his alias of Werner Wagner, which was imperative, so no one would discover his true identity. By sight, Bormann's appearance was totally different now since he had broken his nose in a fall outside his home in Brazil. Also, age had changed his looks considerably, with many wrinkles now running through his skin from the harsh sun of the tropics.

Adolf Stolz was a stern man, versed in the Nazi ideologies, and would carry out any order with binding obedience. He had been a tank commander at the early age of twenty-one in the feared Waffen SS. He fought fiercely for his Fatherland in the battles of the Netherlands and France. Throughout the war, he performed his duty in the Balkan area and into Russia, eventually retreating to Germany in order to guard the Fatherland. After Germany's surrender in 1945, he escaped to the Netherlands and smuggled himself aboard a fishing troller, which brought him to freedom in South America. The Allied Forces had blamed many war atrocities on the Waffen SS, and he wanted to avoid prosecution.

"Herr Stolz, what would you like to drink? It's my treat."

"Very generous of you, Sir," he responded in a pleased manner. "I think a cognac would be in order."

"Very well, Stolz, a commendable choice."

As the waitress retreated to the bar, Bormann glanced back toward Herr Stolz who was admiring the view out the window. He thought well of Adolf. He was a trusted companion and one who had a great deal to do with the endless planning involved in order to achieve their mission.

"Adolf," Bormann said, "do you have your report ready on how things are coming with the migration?"

"Yes, Herr Wagner," he replied with a very military air.

"Adolf, let's dispense with the formalities. Call me Werner, please. We've been friends for too long."

"As you wish, Werner." He lowered his voice considerably. "I am pleased that you think so highly of me, Sir, I mean, Werner. Well, anyway, to get back to the report, as of today, almost ninety percent of the colony has been relocated in Berlin and the surrounding countryside. About twenty-five percent have found jobs within the current population, and the other sixty-five percent have either made their way into the police force, joined the army, or volunteered to track down and capture the scavengers and the sickly people exposed to radiation."

"How serious is the problem with the scavengers, Adolf? Will they pose a threat to our time schedule?"

"Well ..." Adolf sounded unsure of himself, "this is a problem we really didn't outline in our original planning. I have revised our latest reports very stringently, and the fact is the radiation level in the affected areas is five tenths roentgens per hour, which is much too high for normal human inhabitation. My calculations suggest that a person exposed to this level of radiation for one year would receive four thousand roentgens—more than a fatal amount."

Bormann sighed disappointedly.

"What other complications will follow from this unforeseen factor?"

"Sir, as you know, a ten megaton nuclear device hit Bonn and completely destroyed the city and all the inhabitants. The radioactive debris which had been blown up into the stratosphere started to fall. As it fell, it landed north and also northwest of the city. Many of the people in the affected areas were killed instantly. It turned out the aftereffect has been more devastating than even I thought possible. Many people had retreated into underground shelters to escape the fallout, but eventually their food supplies ran low and forced them to venture out and forage for food for themselves and their loved ones. Every time they went outside, they were exposed to more and more of the deadly radiation. As they became literally sick to their stomachs and became too weak to go out anymore, family members were called on to go in their places. The same circumstances prevailed in all cases.

"After everybody became sick and starving because of lack of food, they would venture out of their burrows, dazed by sickness and not even resembling human beings. Bands of affected citizens then ravaged farms and killed their occupants in order to seize desperately needed food, unaware of its contamination. Some died quickly, others were strong enough to stagger on across the countryside, killing and ravaging as they ventured further away from their decimated homes.

"I can honestly say these people are living zombies, Sir, and they have tied up a lot of manpower in order to hunt them down. They are either killed or captured and returned to local hospitals for treatment."

"Adolf, I know this is a very important factor to worry about and should be given a lot of attention, but from what you have just told me, it sounds like half of our problems have vanished."

"What do you mean, Herr Wagner?"

"Well, to the best of my knowledge, the Chancellor, the Bundestag, the Bundesrat, and all the governmental offices of the West German government are located in Bonn, or were. Am I correct?"

"Yes, Sir, you are correct in your statement. But some of the country's major manufacturing plants and mining fields are located in the affected areas also. They will be of no use to us until the year two thousand."

"Damn ...," Bormann whispered under his breath. "What the hell does that mean?"

Adolf stared at him with a very disenchanted look on his face. "Ah ... ah ... this means, Sir, that the iron and steel industry plus the manufacturing power which comes from the Dortmund, Essen, and Duisburg areas, have come to a halt. The coal fields of Cologne, and the surrounding areas are of no value, which will inevitably hurt our chemical industry. Another severe deficit from the loss of the Cologne region is the loss of needed food industries, engineering, and vehicle manufacturing."

Bormann glanced across the table at Adolf sitting and waiting for a reaction to discharge from Bormann.

"Well, Adolf, this information you have just told me is very disturbing. I hope you have some news more inspiring than the last."

"Oh, yes, Herr Wagner, there is much to be thankful for. Even with the loss of the Dortmund region, the overall picture is still very good. Our remaining unaffected regions of Germany can pick up the industrial slack."

"For instance?" Bormann questioned.

"Sir, let me bring you up to date. All of the main German ports are open and operational; this is crucial for our oil supplies, and also for Bremerhaven in the North Sea district. As for our Baltic ports, Wismar and Lubeck remain in fine shape. The most inspiring one, Restock, remains open and the shipbuilding and fishing industries have been virtually unaffected by the past year's events.

"Regarding industrial input and output, the picture still remains a bright one. The deficit in German vehicle production has been taken up by the Opel plant in Russelsheim, the Daimler Benz plant in Stuttgart, and the Volkswagen plant in Wolfsburg. They have been stepping up all their production to offset domestic and worldwide needs.

"As for electric power and steel production, the country's brown coal mining and coke manufacturing has been stepped up to meet future needs. This need for more production has kept places like Lauchhammer, Lusatia, Stalinstadt, Salzgitter, the Soorland, and Volkingen, plus a number of other towns, working very hard to increase production to record levels. Some of the other places which are booming are Frankfurt, Hochst, and Darmstadt, which produce much needed chemicals and pharmaceutical products, and Mannheim, which is famous for chemicals, agricultural machinery, electrical engineering, and shipbuilding. Magdeburg is another place which has been producing agricultural products, potash, coal, timber and heavy machinery at record levels. The East Zone has not been as productive during the past year, but still produces a goodly amount of optical instruments, textiles, paper goods and chemicals.

"The worldwide trade picture has drastically changed for Germany in the past year, also. The elimination of the United States and France from the trade market has been made up for with increased trade with Sweden and the Netherlands. They also landed new markets for their machinery, coal, coke, iron, steel, potash and uranium products in South America and Africa. These new markets have proven most lucrative to our needs.

"As far as the country's food needs, Germany lost several producing regions because of radioactivity, but with the advanced farming technology that the United States has introduced, and the successful collectivization program of agriculture in 1960 which put an end to private farming in the east by the Russians, the food production of Germany has been greatly advanced. We have taken steps to step up the technology in order to overcome the prevailing deficit of fertile land."

"Adolf, Adolf, this is superb news. Things are going right on schedule." Bormann sat back with a more content feeling. "But what is the governmental situation as it stands now? Will we have much trouble swaying people to meet our needs?"

"Herr Wagner, the situation is well in hand. The Federal Republic of Germany, as you brought to my attention, has been virtually eliminated by the destruction of Bonn. The Chancellor and the majority of members in the Bundestag and the Bundesrat were all killed, leaving most of our major cities without proper representation. The only problems we have run into are the remaining members of the party system. The Social Democrats, the Christian Democrats, and the Free Democrats have been trying to rally support for their method of reconstruction."

"Has this been dealt with, Adolf? You know this could set us back if these men have their way."

"Herr Wagner, there is no need to worry. We have sent out assassins from our colony to systematically eliminate the most popular members of this movement."

"Won't this draw suspicion to us, Adolf?"

"I don't think so, since these assassinations are being executed to look like a series of accidents. Besides, with things the way they are today, most people don't have time to be suspicious of everything that's going on. Most people are worried about their own day-to-day survival.

"As for Pankow [the Russian name for Berlin], we have arranged for the name to be changed back to Berlin. The governmental system has been severely interrupted because Russia has pleaded that members of the Volkshammer [known to many as the Rubberstamp Parliament and consisting of the Staatstrat, the State Council, the Ministerrat, and the Executive Branch] be called back to Mother Russia to give leadership in their desperate time of reconstruction.

Even the Politburo [the political bureau which decides the foreign policy, the economy, and had control over the National People's Army, the people's police, and the state security service of East Germany] were called upon to return to Russia. Only a few members were left to control the ever-changing situation."

"How did you start things out in order to give our people the leverage they needed to infiltrate the joint government?" Bormann asked curiously.

"This part of the operation came off even better than I had anticipated from our previous meetings. We sent representatives to infiltrate both East and West, and to advise them that the only firm way to normalize the severe situation at hand was to join forces and work together. They went for that, which surprised me because of the difference in their systems.

"The joint council was made up of equal members of both governments and the affairs were conducted out of the Bundestag. Our members kept hinting around that the government should impose martial law over the country until things started flowing smoothly again. They also advised that the educational system and all instruments of information, including radio stations and the police, should be government controlled to keep things simple and to run as efficiently as possible."

Bormann sat and looked very intently into Adolf's face. "Did they fall for this advice, Adolf?"

"They praised our advice and decided it was the best solution to the situation."

The pressing problems on Bormann's mind having been answered, he stole a quick glance out the window, scanning the surrounding area and noticing the elegant Kurfurstendamm and all the glittering lights that made up that area.

"By the way, Adolf, how has Rudi been doing?"

"You will be pleased to know that he worked his way up in the joint government very quickly because of his good ideas and grasp of the problems at hand. He has gained the respect of all the members of the Bundstag and they treat him with the highest regard. Because of his expertise, and the members' need for positive advice, he is turning out to be a crucial cog in the system. You can be very proud of him, Herr Wagner. He represents all your hard work and devotion."

"When will I be able to see him? Has he missed me?"

"Herr Wagner," Adolf smiled. "Rudi misses you very much and he worries about you a lot because of your ill health. We can go and see him as soon as we leave here. You will be living with him. Max will also be added for security reasons."

"By the way, Adolf," Bormann said curiously, "how has the youth of Germany taken all these changes which both governments have imposed? Do they appear to be suspicious?"

"Quite the opposite, Sir. They have praised the way the government has taken hold of the situation and kept the country from falling apart. The students and the East Germans of the Volksschulen, the Realschule, and the Gymnasium have been taught little about the Nazi era and the reason that the Third Reich was able to come to power. Their teachers have tried to portray the Third Reich as something that happened in a far-off place. This lack of information to the country's youth should give us an added advantage in order to sway the young people to our exact way of thinking."

"Splendid, splendid, Adolf. This report has pleased me very much."

Bormann sat forward in his seat, clinching his fingers together and resting his elbows on the table between them.

"Your memory serves you well as it always has. You have pleased me very much by what I have just heard. I hope that our next meeting is as successful. But for now, I would like to go and meet Rudolf and see how my new quarters are."

"Very well," Adolf replied.

As Bormann rose to put on his coat, he glanced once again over the city that had been the Third Reich and would once again be.

## Chapter 6

20 April 1985

The trees and beautifully colored flowers dotting the streets whisked by as our taxi sped quickly down the road toward the inner center of Berlin. I couldn't help but ponder the fact that this bright, energetic city was once the breeding ground for the devastation and misery which had kept Simon and myself busy for nearly forty years.

The past year had been crazy and disorganized. I had spent most of my time in Vermont taking care of Simon, who had gone into a severe state of depression after the news of Itka's death. He needed constant observation and care which could only be accomplished by me, since most medical facilities were overcrowded with people who had come down with radiation sickness or even worse. It had taken most of my energy to convince Simon that this crisis should only strengthen our reasons for doing what we do. The people who had caused this catastrophe must be tracked down and stopped.

The situation, as it stood in the world, was one of utter chaos. Millions of people had been killed by the nuclear explosions and accompanying radiation. Many others were sick and starving, with no medical personnel or supplies to take care of their needs. The U.S. government and military might had been practically eliminated.

Only the officials and troops which had been kept several hundred feet underground in secret military installations, specifically designed in the event of a nuclear attack, remained alive. The country did its best to pick up the pieces and start over, but too much destruction and death had already occurred. Most of the military troops had been sent out to kill any looters and to find and take care of people who had been affected by the intense radiation levels from the explosions.

The worst problem of all was the question of how to feed the remaining population. Most agricultural centers of the U.S., which had been responsible for the main food staples in the past, were now inadequate to plant crops; radiation levels were too high to sustain any healthy crops. Most of the food which kept Americans alive was flown in from Canada, that country being virtually untouched by nuclear explosions and spreading radiation from the United States.

Canada's government and military troops had offered and given much assistance since that day of destruction, and without it, the United States would have probably ceased to exist.

The worldwide situation was good in some spots and bad in others. Russia had been totally devastated by the United States' retaliatory strikes on the country. Their situation had been further complicated because all their population centers had been hit by explosions.

Russia's neighbor, China, had been covered by deadly radiation and could not offer any assistance. Both countries were totally helpless and their capability to be world powers had ended.

Japan, Britain, and France had been hit by Russian nuclear strikes or misguided missiles, which left these key military and economic countries in a state of confusion. Some countries nearby were lending assistance, but progress was slow and there was much work to be done.

As for the rest of the world, except for some high radiation levels in places, they were merely existing and carrying on as best they could.

World trade had to be restructured because of the elimination of several important countries. Germany had been leading the other countries as far as organizing and carrying out the inner workings of the complex commerce system. Most of the nations were very pleased and confident that Germany was handling things well since they had been the strongest European country economically before the nuclear war had begun. Most world leaders would follow German ideas and plans as confidently as their own religion.

This state of affairs had made me even more nervous than I already was about the resurgence of the German Nazi party. I had kept a close eye on the Canadian newspapers in order to see how fast Germany was building up industrial and military might. From all indications, it had the same pattern as that of the buildup in the last part of the 1930s. From the information that I had attained from Herman, and that which I had already been reading, I couldn't help but think that the gears of the Nazi party had begun to turn again.

Recently, Simon was beginning to show improvement and was starting to recover from his depressed state. The only means by which I could achieve this was to convince him that he must avenge his sister's murder and make the murderers pay for the misery they had caused the world. This, and only this, kept him going from one day to another.

Our financial status was one which we had not been used to for quite some time. Itka's money had been stored in a bank in downtown Manhattan and was destroyed in the bombings. With the death of Itka and the loss of her money, we were virtually broke. The government kept us sheltered and supplied with food, but we had nothing of value to our names except two beautiful gold watches which Itka had given us for our birthdays a few years ago. Regretfully, we decided to sell them in order to attain enough money to purchase two airline tickets from Montreal to Tegel airport in Berlin.

As we traveled along toward the nucleus of Berlin, I noticed a Jewish community center posted in a tourist pamphlet which I had picked up at the airport. I instructed the taxi driver to go to the corner of Kurfurstendamm and Fasanenstrasse where the center was located, some two kilometers from our present position.

Our religious participation had diminished in past years because of the irregularity of our business. Now, with our situation being very different, we decided to stop in to visit for a while and ask for guidance during these trying times. I would have to admit that I was very weak in my Hebrew and religious readings, which I had excelled in as a boy.

As the taxi slowed to a stop, I noticed a brown and beige marble building with several pots of beautiful pink roses out front. We paid the driver his fare and then he hurried off in his taxi. Simon and I approached the glass revolving door which led into the synagogue. As we pushed our way through, I looked up and noticed a woman coming out of the building. She was a very attractive woman who appeared to be in her early fifties. She had long black hair down to her shoulders and was wearing a beautiful pink and red short-sleeved dress with black shoes. For some unknown reason, I felt that I knew this woman from some place in the past. As she started down the steps, I pushed my way around to the outside. I felt that I had to say something, but if I was wrong ... how embarrassing it would be.

She stopped at a pot of those beautiful roses and bent over to smell their elegant fragrance.

"Fraulein," I called in a conservative voice.

She turned and looked at me, not startled by my call.

"Do I know you from somewhere?" I asked politely. Our eyes exchanged glances for a second, but no reaction was forthcoming.

"I'm not sure, Sir. Are you a native Berliner?" She had a soft, meek voice.

"No, I'm from the United States, but originally from Poland."

Her eyes began to light up with joy and a slight smile came to her face.

"From Poland?" she said in a questioning voice. "What part?"

"Radom, Fraulein. I lived there until I was deported to a work camp by the Nazis in 1939."

The look in her eyes was first one of sadness but then turned to joy.

"Saul? Is your name Saul Weinberg?" she asked in an uplifting voice.

"Yes, yes it is. How do you know me?"

Simon had walked outside wondering what had enticed my curiosity. He now stood beside me.

"Saul, I'm surprised at you. Wasn't it you who told me I would always be the only girl in your heart?"

She stood there looking at me, waiting for some sort of positive reaction. All of a sudden Simon stepped forward and said, "Judith Barelkousky, is that you?"

She began to laugh. "Yes, Simon, it is I."

"Judith, Judith," I broke into the conversation. "It's been so long. How have you been? How did you come to live in Berlin? Are you visiting?"

As I spewed out the questions, I grasped her hands and kissed her on the cheek affectionately.

"Saul, please," she said, "one question at a time."

"I'm sorry, Judith, but I am so overwhelmed by running into a friendly face such as yours ...well ...I'm almost speechless."

"That doesn't sound like the Saul Weinberg I used to know," she responded gingerly. "You seemed to always have a sweet thing to say to me, just to keep me wondering about you."

Simon broke out in a bit of a chuckle.

"By the way, Simon, how have you been since I saw you last?" Judith asked, curiously.

"Well, ah ..., well, ah ...," Simon struggled. "Not bad, Judith. How has life been treating you?"

"Very well, Simon. I have made a decent life here in Berlin, and since the nuclear war restrictions on travel have been lifted, I can go anywhere I please without answering to anyone. But enough about me, how have you two detectives been?"

"How do you know what we do?" Simon snapped at Judith.

"Simon, Simon, calm yourself down," I said.

"I'm sorry to have taken you by surprise," Judith explained, "but after the news from Haifa of the Eichmann capture in 1960, you two men became very famous. After that, it was fairly reasonable to assume that you hunted Nazis for a living."

"Are you dissatisfied with us because of our life's occupation?"

I waited nervously for an answer.

"Quite the opposite, Saul. I believe in what you are doing and respect both you and Simon for your devotion to achieving justice for the Jewish people. Shortly after the war, my mother and father wrote me a letter from Radom and informed me that your parents had been killed at the Treblinka Death Camp and that your whereabouts were unknown. All I could think of was that you were dead also."

"How did you and your family survive?" I questioned. "I lost contact with you a couple of weeks before we were taken by train to the work camp. Where did you go? How did you escape?" I asked, realizing I was again bombarding her with questions.

"My mother and father and I escaped out of Radom by cover of darkness one night," Judith explained with an undaunted look on her face.

"I had no idea we were even leaving until my father came to me and said to get ready. We left the house in a matter of minutes. Once we were out of the city, we sometimes hitched rides with local farmers on the backs of their carts, but mainly we ventured on foot through fields and across streams. The journey took an awful toll on my father, but he knew we must get away from all the misery and pain that was to come.

"We eventually reached the city of Kiev in the Ukraine, but we stayed there for only a couple of months because a variety of rumors were filtering east concerning the dreaded Einsatzgruppe mobile death squads, run by the worst enemy to the Jewish people, Adolf Eichmann.

"People were literally being dragged out of their homes by the hundreds and brought to nearby mass grave sites for execution. Those mothers who put up a fight risked getting smashed by the butt end of a rifle or having their child shot or crushed right in front of their eyes. These murderers also weren't very particular about who was shot, whether it was a Jewish family or a band of Gypsies in the area, or even the mentally ill.

"I remember many nights while talking over dinner, my father would say dozens of times, 'When will these maniacs be stopped? When will the nightmare cease?' I was old enough to realize the seriousness of what was occurring, and it made me shiver sometimes when I was trying to go to sleep.

"Before long, the stories filtered back that several hundred people had been massacred in the city of Rouno, near Poland. My father decided that we should make the long journey all the way to Stalingrad, in order to be safe for the duration of the war. Before we left, my father tried to persuade the local Jewish people to flee with us. His efforts were mostly in vain … only a few people came along. I could never understand why the Jews never thought they would be harmed, especially after hearing of all the atrocities not far from their own homes.

"After the fighting had ceased and the war had ended, my parents returned to Radom as did I. The stories and sadness that were brought back to our home and town were unbearable. The friends and loved ones I once had as a child were never to return. I had to get out of Radom to keep my peace of mind.

"My parents were very understanding and bid me their best. Not too long after, I ventured off to Heidelberg to attend the university and with the hope of receiving a degree in Art Science. I had always loved art as a child and dreamed that I would someday attend. But you two should know that better than anyone, since I had to help you two students fake your way through the finer points of art. Do you remember?"

"I sure do," Simon exclaimed, chuckling. "I never had a chance when it came to art. I remember one night Itka was tutoring me on the subject ...."

Simon stopped right in the middle of his sentence. A mournful look came to his face. Judith called "Simon, Simon, what's the matter? Simon, did I say something wrong?"

A few moments passed before Simon lifted his head.

"My sister was killed in New York when the nuclear war started." Simon forced the words out.

"I'm sorry, Simon," Judith said, comforting him. "Itka was a nice girl and a very devoted friend. I shall remember her always."

"So will I," Simon agreed, kicking a small stone around with his foot, trying to hold back his tears.

I decided to change the subject in order to brighten up the atmosphere.

"Judith, please continue with your story. I'm very interested in your college escapades."

"Well, there's not that much to tell, Saul," Judith exclaimed. "My life was not a very exciting one, mostly because I had a limited amount of money to pay for my schooling and my living expenses. What I had was earned working after classes in the school library.

# The Descendant

Between my job and school in the day, then studying at night, my social life was virtually nonexistent. I studied long, hard hours, but it finally gained me recognition by one of my professors. This eventually led to my present job here in Berlin, as an art expert at one of the local museums. Since 1951, I have lived here in a room which I am renting from a local baker and his wife."

"Has your social life changed any?" I questioned as a slight twinge of jealousy came to my mind.

"No, not really, Saul. I've led a simple life and most of my friends and acquaintances have been through the museum. I guess I've been sort of a loner most of my life and probably spend too much time at my job. My social life as it stands now consists of mostly traveling around Europe from time to time during the year, and maybe going down to the Tiergarten to relax and enjoy the scenery and watch the boats and people ... but most of all just to get away from my daily routine."

Judith paused for a moment and let out an exasperated breath.

"Well, enough about me. What has brought you two to Berlin anyway?"

Simon and I looked at each other simultaneously, wondering what to say.

"Well, Judith, it's sort of a long story," I began. "One which we can fill you in on later. Right now, we could use some advice."

"What is it, Saul?" she asked.

"We need a suggestion on an inexpensive place to stay and maybe a job of some sort."

"You mean you have nothing at all left?" She looked at us with a puzzled look.

"We lost all we had during the war," I explained, "but we need just enough to get by on."

Judith thought for a moment, then a smile came to her face.

"I know ... I've got a great idea. My landlord, Herr Schmidt, has been trying to rent two rooms upstairs from his bakery, and as a matter-of-fact, he is looking for part-time help down in the bakery. I'm sure we could work something out with him."

Judith had a very excited look on her face. One which I had seen many times when I was younger. Simon and I agreed to Judith's offer and escorted her to her home, which was not far from the Jewish center.

********

As I lay in my bed gazing out the window to the south of Berlin, I couldn't help but think about all the horror and misery the world had undergone in the past year. Why had it happened? Was our information really reliable? Maybe I was grasping for something that wasn't really happening. I supposed those questions couldn't really be answered until we had a chance to talk to some local people in the government. But then again, suppose it was genuinely happening? Who was in this horrible conspiracy? Was it happening now or in the near future? Whom could we trust, and whom could we not trust? These questions were alarming. At least we had a place to stay and one of us had a job.

My thoughts then drifted off to Ludwig Schmidt and his wife, Gretta. The Schmidts dealt with a large volume of people, but were able to keep a personal touch which kept the customers happy.

Ludwig and Gretta were natives of Berlin and had lived through the horrors of World War II. They both vividly remembered Hitler's regime and were very negative about the Nazis and their terrible tactics to exterminate the Jews and conquer the world.

Ludwig Schmidt was a proud man who believed in hard work and honesty in order to prosper in life. He stood about six feet tall with a normal build and was in his early sixties. He was a nice man who cared about others, and this was sincerely evident by the way he had taken us in and by the way he took to Judith as his own daughter.

Ludwig had been a Gerfreiter in the Wehrmacht during the war. He was strongly against the beliefs and tactics brought on by the Nazi regime, but feared for his loving wife if he should speak out against Hitler. He fought bravely until the end came for Germany, which was a welcome thought. The Russians took him prisoner in a building overlooking the Spree River, where he and a handful of other comrades had been sent to pin down oncoming Communist troops crossing a badly damaged bridge into the heart of Berlin.

Gretta Schmidt was a beautiful woman in her late fifties with long blonde hair, put up in a bun, and had very high cheek bones which made her very attractive for her age.

When they first met, Saul noticed she talked with a severe stutter in her voice, which cued his curiosity because of her intelligent nature. Judith later informed him that Frau Schmidt had been raped several times by members of the Russian 220th Guard Regiment, which went from house to house interrogating civilians and tracking down snipers from the surrounding buildings. She had also been beaten severely because of her strong will not to give in to the soldiers. Ludwig vowed he would track down the men responsible for this fiendish act and kill them. Fearing he would be killed, Gretta had dissuaded Ludwig from this plan of action.

I was taken away from my thoughts by a knock at the door. I knew it could not be Simon because he looked so tired when we retired after dinner for the night, I knew he would sleep soundly.

"Come in," I said with a note of curiosity.

The door creaked as it opened. A figure entered the room.

"I just thought I would come in and check to see if everything was all right, Saul."

From the sound of the voice, I knew it was Judith.

"Well, Judith, I'm flattered about the room service I'm getting," I complimented.

She began to laugh in a low voice. "That's quite all right, Sir."

She sat down on the edge of the bed and I could see her radiant face as it appeared in the moonlight shining through the window. Judith was such a beautiful woman and still resembled the quiet little girl I had had a crush on when I was a young man.

"Saul, I'm scared," she said bending over and throwing her hands around my neck. I sat up straight in order to comfort her. I could feel her heart pulsating against my chest.

"If this story you and Simon have told me is true, you could put yourself in great danger by interfering."

I put my hands around Judith's waist and looked into her eyes.

"Judith, we must try to find out if any of this information is true," I said in a stern voice. "If something like this ever got started, who knows what could happen. Judith," I spoke in a consoling voice, "Simon and I are experienced in these matters and we have the knowledge and knowhow to find these maniacs and stop them."

"But, Saul," Judith raised her hand, brushing away a rolling tear, "who can you trust? How will you know the person you talk to is not a loyal Nazi or a civilian sympathetic with their movement to take over?"

"Judith, please, just trust me for now. Besides, we should forget about this until tomorrow anyway and get some rest."

Judith gazed into my eyes and I into hers. I could see a silhouette of myself reflecting from the pools of tears in her eyes. She leaned forward, pressing her lips firmly on mine. I remembered back for a second to the picnics we used to go on in the forest. Judith kissed me the same way then, always being the aggressor.

We kissed passionately. Judith stood up from the edge of the bed, facing me, still looking into my eyes. With her left hand she began unbuttoning her beautiful white nightgown, eventually shedding it to the floor. Her naked body was in full view by the beaming light from the moon. She was a thoroughly beautiful creature and all I had imagined when I was a younger man back in Radom.

Judith stepped forward, caressing her hand through my hair and resting my head into her breasts. I put my perspiring hands on Judith's thighs and directed her body down onto the bed. I removed my own clothes then and our two bodies embraced with such strength that I wished this moment could last forever. Judith was such a loving and caring person and one who enjoyed life to its fullest.

## Chapter 7

22 July 1985

The green Mercedes moved swiftly down the road with the slight hum of a diesel engine in the background. It was a relaxing journey, and one which Bormann had looked forward to. The hard work and preparations that had gone into the past few months had taken its toll on his health. He realized that his days with the Fuhrer had also taken much of his time and energy, but all of the toil and trouble had been worth the effort. Rudi sat beside him in the back seat, with his head nudged slightly against the side of the seat, catching some sleep on their journey.

These past months had been such hard work for Rudi, helping around the Reichstag and jockeying for more lucrative positions in the party. He looked so peaceful with his eyes closed, unknowing of his real future and the endless responsibility it would draw from his body and mind.

Hans was in the front of the car, busy concentrating on his driving skills. As always, he was doing his job just perfectly, but the beautiful sights of the southern German countryside were enough to take anyone's mind off the road. The green fields and the snow-capped mountains in the distance were so beautiful, he thought that nowhere else in the world had he ever seen such magnificent scenery.

They had been driving for quite some time and were now thirty-five kilometers southwest of Munich. This city had played host to many foreign dignitaries before and during the war. Bormann would usually confer with the Fuhrer at nearby Berchtesgaden, then retire back to a hotel room in the city at night; occasionally he was invited to stay at Hitler's mountainside retreat, called the "Berghof."

The Fuhrer was a master of foreign affairs and knew exactly how to play people against each other. He would also keep them off balance by not telling them just what he was thinking. This skill was evident as the Fuhrer planned the invasion of Poland in 1939, the name of the plan being called "Operation Himmler." This diabolical scheme had been thought up by the Chief of the SS Security Service himself, Reinhard Heydrich. He and his cohorts would eventually carry out their most important mission of the Final Solution as the war continued. He had a cunning plan to make it look as if Poland were the aggressor against Germany. He believed that Poland provided necessary living space for the German people.

The plan entailed having SD detachments disguised as Polish soldiers stir up incidents along the border the night before the invasion was to begin. During that time, they would attack a forestry station, a customs building, and occupy, for a brief time, the radio station at Gleiwitz. In the radio station men would shout anti-German slogans into the microphone and then retreat, leaving behind a number of dead bodies. Even the bodies presented no real problem. Heydrich had already picked his victims from a nearby concentration camp.

As their car came to a bend in the road, Bormann noticed a large branch from a tree lying across the road ahead. Hans brought the car to a halt, stopping very near the branch. Bormann glanced around and noticed that there was no tree from which the branch could have broken; all that was around was tall green grass in a field next to them. Hans turned around to ask for his thoughts, but he just shrugged his shoulders.

All of a sudden, a rock was hurled from the grass at the passenger side window, smashing it into tiny pieces. Bormann peered off into the grassy field and noticed a band of men and a few women lunging toward their car. They had a crazed look in their eyes and their faces were so hideous, he could not believe what he was seeing. Most of them were very unstable on their feet and some were almost crawling on their hands and knees toward the car. As Bormann turned to his right to check the back side of the car, a monstrous face appeared against the window. He jerked his head back from the sudden shock. The man was pulling on the door handle, trying to open it, but it was locked. His body was so scarred that he looked as if he had been in a fire. The hair on his head was virtually gone. There were red and purple veins running through his face, and in many places on his face and arms the skin had slid like melted cheese, leaving behind bleeding sores and exposed bone.

Rudi was awakened by all the excitement.

"Father," Rudi shouted, "who are these monstrous people? What do they want with us?"

"I don't know, Rudi," Bormann responded nervously.

Bormann's hands became very sweaty as he kept them pushed on the door lock.

"Hans," he shouted, "get rid of these beasts. Kill them before they get into the car."

Hans responded without saying a word. He pulled a pistol from a holster under his left arm and pushed the button down for the electric window. One of the beasts grabbed Hans by the shoulders and began shaking him. He managed to raise his gun and fire point blank into the man's stomach. The man flew back and fell to the road.

By this time almost twenty of the beasts had come to the side of the car. Hans opened his door and stepped out quickly. Before he could fire again, another beast jumped on his back and tried to wrestle him to the ground.

Both Rudi and Bormann were helpless because they were unarmed. Bormann looked at Rudi. His face was tense, and his fear was evident.

Hans managed to overcome his assailant and throw him off. He raised his pistol again and fired, killing the aggressor.

With the thirst to kill in their eyes, the people on the other side of the auto began trying to overturn the car. As Bormann and Rudi sat there, the car began to shake back and forth, but the car was not even being lifted off the ground. These people's strength had greatly diminished from a lack of food and because of radiation sickness.

It was a miracle how a band of these zombies could live so long. Hans had managed to overcome a few more people while the gang was still shaking the car. He came around to the hood of the car and began to fire. People were dropping like flies. All Bormann could hear was screaming and moaning coming from outside. The rest of the zombies turned and ran back into the high green grassy fields.

Hans backed up into the car and began wiping the sweat from his forehead. He was visibly shaken by the incident.

Rudi and Bormann unlocked their doors and emerged from the car.

"Hans, are you all right?" Rudi asked.

Hans turned around.

"I'm all right, Rudi," he forced out, still panting.

"Here, here, you come and sit down, Hans. You're lucky to be alive."

Hans sat down on the pavement resting his head up against the tire. Bormann stood next to Hans, looking down at him. "Hans, what in hell happened? I thought the police and army had these bomb victims under control."

Bormann stood there tense and excited, waiting for a reply.

Rudi interjected. "Father, come now, we can't expect them to round up all these scavengers overnight. They are doing the best they can."

Hans looked up at Bormann with a boyish look on his face, apparently glad that Rudi had come to his defense.

"Hans, I'm sorry I got upset with you, but these scavengers gave me such a scare."

He began to pat Hans on the shoulder.

"That's all right, Sir," he replied confidently. "As soon as we get back from Berchtesgaden, I will look into the matter in some depth."

Rudi jumped in, "I will also help him, Father, but for now I think we should continue our trip."

Bormann put his hand out to Hans and pulled him up to his feet.

"And so we shall," he said.

********

As they traveled down the Alpine Road into the little town of Berchtesgaden, Bormann noticed the twin steeples of the Augustinian Abbey, originally built in the Twelfth Century. Off in the distance were the snow-capped Bavarian Alps, with the twin peaks of Hochkalter and Waltzman.

How Bormann had anticipated seeing the Berghof again. He had not been to Hitler's mountain retreat in more than forty years. So much of his time had been devoted to this beautiful spot in the past. His mind wandered back to the days when this place had meant so much to Hitler and how it had come to be.

********

The Berghof came into existence in 1925, just after Hitler had emerged from prison. He rented a quaint cottage in the remote Bavarian village of Obersalzberg, which was three thousand feet above Berchtesgaden. He would escape there when he had some serious thinking to do.

The Fuhrer finally wished to purchase the property around this fine place, which consisted of the Berghof property, a few fields, and a small parcel of woods. By purchasing many titles of land in the years that followed, he managed to expand his property to ten square kilometers of woodland and eighty hectares of farmland. Much of this land was used to grow the Fuhrer's vegetables, since he was a strict vegetarian.

By the summer of 1936, the first expansion of the Berghof was completed. This was important, since this home would accommodate many people. The new structure was four times its original size and contained some thirty rooms. Through the hallway entrance and to the left was a huge living and conference room to entertain dignitaries from their country and foreign nations. On the second floor, the Fuhrer's living room, bedroom and office were situated, with his mistress Eva Braun's room a few steps down to the rear.

No expense had been spared in renovating the great mansion: the window panes were framed in lead; there were marble columns in the halls; and the furniture was a combination of genuine antiques.

As time moved on, the Berghof had to be expanded to include a huge garage for all the Fuhrer's staff cars, and he needed barracks to house the Reich Security Service and the Leibstandarte, which was in charge of security.

One of the most extravagant construction plans, called the Kehlstein, had been designed by Bormann. This was to be a birthday present for the Fuhrer. It was nicknamed the Teahouse and sat on a rock six thousand feet above the mansion.

# The Descendant

By the fall of 1938, the Kehlstein was finally finished at the cost of over thirty million reichsmarks. It was a beautiful piece of construction.

One day in September of that year, Bormann and the Fuhrer decided to inspect the Teahouse. They were driven up a steep, winding road to a point which was fifty-six hundred feet above sea level. They then traveled through a brightly lit, solid rock tunnel and ended up at a shiny brass elevator which took them four hundred more feet to the top. The house contained a big kitchen, dining room, study, guard room, bathrooms, cellars, a terrace, and the big room which was circular with a huge fireplace. There was also a panorama of picture windows which offered a magnificent view.

Hitler was excited about the Teahouse and wanted to show it off to everyone. The Fuhrer took Goebbels, Himmler, and a noted British journalist, Ward Price, for a tour; Price later nicknamed the Teahouse the "Eagle's Nest."

Many dignitaries toured the Teahouse also. They included Gauleiter of Munich, Adolf Wagner and the Prince of Hesse, and the French Ambassador, Andre Francois-Poncet, a man with whom the Fuhrer enjoyed conversing immensely.

Bormann enjoyed the Teahouse himself to entertain a lady friend or to have an undisturbed talk with a party official whom he was trying to feel out.

Bormann's life with the Fuhrer was a never-ending dream, to be as efficient an Aryan servant as possible.

The Fuhrer usually arose from bed around noon, and by the time the mid-day briefing session was over with and his generals had brought him up to date on the war, it was close to four p.m.

About this time his mistress, Eva, would make her appearance with her two dogs. The Fuhrer would have to transform from Head of State to a jovial host. (Eva and Bormann never really got along, but they managed to keep out of each other's way. In his opinion, all she cared about was being a socialite and which friends she could invite to impress with her lavish house.)

By this time, everyone was ready to sit for lunch. This usually consisted of sauerbraten and the Fuhrer would eat his vegetarian meals cooked by one of his many doctors at the Berchtesgaden Clinic. The meals were transported to the Berghof kitchen for heating.

While lunch was going on, Bormann's duties as Reichslieter never stopped. He remembered, on many occasions, being called away from the table to transact some urgent business in Berlin or to locate some information that the Fuhrer wanted immediately.

After lunch they would go out on their twenty minute walk and eventually end up at the lower Teahouse, a round stone building located below the Berghof. From this room was a magnificent view of the Ach River flowing down the countryside, and also the Baroque Towers of Salzburg.

At seven p.m., a band of vehicles would arrive at the mountain retreat and more business would have to be handled. This time was taken to talk with foreign dignitaries or to discuss pending domestic affairs.

Two hours later the Fuhrer would sit for dinner. The conversation usually consisted of stories, many of which were about the Fuhrer's youth. The atmosphere was gay and informal.

Immediately after the evening military conference, they would all retire to the living room to sit by the fireplace and relax in the semidarkness. By this time many of the people were tired and would tend to drift off into sleep during one of the Fuhrer's lectures on the evils of tobacco or liquor. Bormann would usually be very attentive unless something important came up and he had to leave.

As the car pulled up in front of the Berghof, an empty feeling came to mind. The building had been completely destroyed, but was now restored to a point, it being one of Germany's most popular tourist attractions. Bormann saw many tour guides and group parties roaming the area, taking pictures, and viewing the sites.

Hans stepped from the car to open Bormann's door.

"Thank you, Hans," he replied. "Well, what do you think?"

"Sir, I don't like it as much as the original. Even my barracks have disappeared over there," Hans added.

Bormann gave Hans an evil stare alerting him to the fact that they were supposed to be sightseers.

"Father, this view is fantastic," Rudi then said excitedly. "It is like nothing I've ever seen in my entire life."

"I'm glad you're enjoying it, Rudi."

Bormann escorted him over to the edge of the pavement.

"Son, do you see that patch of green grass over there?" he asked in a low tone of voice. "An elderly couple used to live there at one time. One day, the Fuhrer and I were standing here and he told me that he thought the house spoiled the view. So, being the devoted worker I was, I contacted the couple one day while the Fuhrer was away and offered them a check for several reichsmarks to buy their home. We finally came to an agreement and by the time the Fuhrer came back, I had already torn the house down and replaced it with grass and several grazing cows."

"Was the Fuhrer surprised, Father?" Rudi asked.

"He was ecstatic. I remember he couldn't stop talking about it for hours."

"You must have found great satisfaction in making the Fuhrer happy."

"I did, Rudi, I did. One day the Fuhrer said he trusted me more than most because I had spent time in prison as had he."

"I didn't know that, Father," Rudi said inquisitively.

"Oh yes, Rudi. I spent over a year in prison for my part in the killing of a Communist spy named Walter Kadow. He had managed to join our antisemitic organization and was found out by one of our members. He was exterminated one night after he left a tavern."

"How dare that lousy Bolshevik try to join and undermine your organization, Father!" Rudi barked out.

"Don't worry, Rudi. We had our ways to handle things in those days. Not like the way people have done things since. I wonder where Hans has drifted off to, Rudi?" Bormann asked. "We should be leaving if we are to eat supper and return to Berlin by evening."

As Bormann turned around, he noticed Hans taking a picture of a lovely German couple who looked to be on their honeymoon. It gave Bormann's heart a good feeling to see a good, healthy, German couple. They would need all the people they could get to continue the triumphant Fourth Reich.

## Chapter 8

23, July, 1985

As I walked up the steps of the Reichstag Government Building, the sun glared down brightly on the old stone structure. It was a beautiful day, but I would have rather packed a picnic lunch and taken Judith for a walk in the Tiergarten Park. She was such an attractive woman. In just the short time we had spent together, the love I had felt in my younger days seemed to be rekindled.

    I did my share of the work at the bakery, but a good many hours were spent with Judith, leaving Simon alone to contend with the memories of his sister's death. The Schmidts understood the situation and treated Simon gently and with kindness. As Simon's work at the bakery was only part-time, he was able to inquire around Berlin for some kind of clue as to what was happening. I managed also to equal Simon's time and efforts of investigation. Thus, we were each accomplishing our primary goal.

    I held the big brass door for a man walking out of the entrance and then stepped into the lobby of the Reichstag. The hallways were buzzing with the sound of people scurrying here and there. It was just as I had pictured a place of government to be. The red and black marble walls stretched eight meters high to a ceiling with two huge crystal chandeliers. The floors were made of black and white tile that looked as if they were polished daily.

I stepped over to the receptionist's desk to locate the room number of the Nazi Criminal Affairs Division. There was a pretty blonde-haired girl there who directed me to the hallway, then five doors down on the left. I thanked her and walked away leisurely, thumbing through my file folder on Martin Bormann. It contained some two hundred pages of information concerning the Reichslieter. I looked over Bormann's family history, quickly moving on to his personal history. I wanted to be sure I knew what I was talking about before I dropped my bit of information in some German bureaucrat's lap.

Suddenly, I collided with someone who was also walking down the corridor, but coming from the opposite direction. I glanced up quickly to find a man standing there. He seemed to be looking straight down at my folder. I closed it quickly, wondering if he had seen the identifying picture and the name at the top. He gave me a puzzled look, said, "Excuse me," and then moved on.

A chilling feeling went up my spine as I became paranoid by my surroundings. How could I be so stupid? For all I knew, this diabolical plot to revive the Third Reich could have started already.

Oh, I thought to myself. Could it possibly be that the man was in on the plot? If so, will he then tell others about me? What am I to do?

I stood there in the hallway like a little boy who had just lost his mother.

"This is ridiculous," I whispered ever so softly. "I am the aggressor and Simon and I have to bring these murderers to justice. The professional training that I have had over the years is more than adequate to keep me alive and alert at all times."

I stood up straight, and a wave of confidence seemed to enter my body. As I turned to walk on, I noticed the office I was looking for was right in front of me. I opened the door and walked into a beautifully furnished office. Inside was a man standing in front of a filing cabinet, looking down into it. I seemed to startle him.

"Oh ... oh, hello. May I help you?" he blurted out, obviously surprised.

"Well, I hope so," I responded, in an important-sounding manner. "My name is Saul Weinberg of the Jewish Liberation League, working out of Haifa, Israel."

I thought that would impress him.

"Well, well," he said politely. "Have a seat Herr Weinberg, and I will be with you in just a moment. I'm looking for a file but I'm just not having any luck finding it."

He stuck his head back into the filing cabinet and began flipping folders.

I sat down in a plush-looking, brown leather chair and glanced around the office. The furnishings were expensive and showed excellent taste. The room consisted of a large handcrafted desk facing me, with a picture of Chancellor Bismark hanging from the wall in back of it. There were also several filing cabinets and microfilm cabinets at various places around the room.

As I looked downward, I noticed hardwood floors with a huge Ming Oriental rug covering most of the floor.

I reached over to the table beside me and picked up a copy of the local Berlin paper. The headline read, "Leading Social Democrat Killed in Tragic Accident." I read down into the fine print. It said a man by the name of Karl Frahm had been driving home late at night and had fallen asleep at the wheel. He slammed into a utility pole and was killed instantly. No one witnessed the accident, but the cause was not questioned. I threw the paper back on the end table and looked up.

"Did you know this man who was killed?" I questioned.

"Who? Karl?" he responded. "Sure. Everybody knew Karl. He was one of those people in government with real charisma ... you know what I mean?"

I nodded my head.

"A hell of a nice guy, too. Boy does he have an interesting background."

"What do you mean?" I asked.

"Well, originally, in 1933, he was exiled by the Nazi Party to Scandinavia because of his political beliefs. But that couldn't keep old Karl down. H showed up as a press agent at the Nuremburg trials in 1945. After that, he entered the Bundestag as an observer deputy from West Berlin, and at that time he was only thirty-six years old. Since then, he has held several key posts in the Social Democratic Party as a key debater and he was even the Mayor of Berlin in 1957. He also wrote several books on a variety of different subjects."

"He does sound very impressive," I admitted.

"He sure was," the man looked up scratching his chin. "You know, it's funny ...."

"What's funny?" I asked.

"Well, Karl just wasn't the kind of guy you would pick to fall asleep behind the wheel of an auto. He was such a safe driver."

"Was there any suspicious information reported about the accident?" I questioned.

"There was one thing I noticed in the official report. It said that the driver's door and front fender were smashed in and blue paint was left on the door. At first the police thought it might have been a drunk driver, or someone else that had forced him off the road. But this proved to be untrue."

"Why was that?"

"A man from the Reichstag Security Office told the police he had noticed the dent in Karl's car the same day in the parking lot. The police had no reason to dispute the information since the man parked right next to Karl every day."

My suspicious mind began to crank up as an engine in motion.

"Was there any reason someone would want to have Herr Frahm killed?"

"I don't think so. The only friction he has had lately was with the provisional government. A lot of members are against the government's controlling the press, the radio, and the television stations until the Reconstruction Period has become somewhat more stable. Karl was very upset with the way things had been going because of the structure of our government now compared to the rise of the Nazi Party to power in the 1930s."

A bell went off in my head when I heard this. Could my suspicions be right? Was this awful plot already in progress? I'd have to investigate Martin Bormann before I did anything else. I tried to calm the butterflies inside of my stomach so I could tell my story convincingly.

"Who are these people that would want such a thing?" I blurted out, somewhat rudely.

"They are loyal Germans, just like any other citizen," he defended. "You have to realize, Herr Weinberg, most of the key party members were killed in Bonn last year by the war. These people have given their best effort to try to normalize the country with limited personnel and also begin an extensive recruiting program."

"I'm sorry, Herr, Herr ..." I hesitated.

"My name is Alfred Klopfer. In all the excitement, I neglected to introduce myself," he apologized.

"That's quite all right, Herr Klopfer. Why don't we get down to the business at hand?"

"Which is?" he asked with a serious expression.

"Herr Klopfer, as bizarre as this may seem, I have up-to-date information that proves Martin Bormann is still alive."

A smile crossed his face.

"Saul ... may I call you Saul?"

"Yes, by all means," I agreed.

"Our information, which is backed up by several people in responsible positions, proves Martin Bormann is dead. His body was dug up on December 8, 1972, on the Ulap Fairgrounds by two workers who were moving electric power conduits in preparation for new construction. Why do you people from Haifa persist in going around chasing ghosts? I have files and more files on legitimate Nazi war criminals for whom you could be looking." He began picking up clumps of files and dropping them back down on his desk. "Do you want to make a name for yourself back in Israel, or just get a cover story in some magazine?"

"That is not true!" I shouted back at him. "I am a loyal Jew doing a job that most people would rather forget. My whole adult life has been spent running all over the world trying to bring as many of these maniacs to trial as possible. For your information, both my parents died in German extermination centers and my efforts are devoted and thoroughly unselfish."

Herr Klopfer slid back into his highly polished leather chair and interweaved his fingers.

"Well, Saul. I'll tell you what we can do."

"What?" I answered disgustedly.

"First I will pull the file on Martin Bormann and go over it with you. When I am finished, if you are not satisfied that this is your man, then I will listen to your story. Fair enough?"

I thought for a moment and decided to be more tactful.

"Okay, Herr Klopfer. You win."

I stepped behind the desk as he scanned through a big gray filing cabinet for Bormann's case folder. Eventually he emerged with a brown folder with the code V4-88-537 typed on a white label. He placed it down in front of me and opened it.

"Remember, as I dictate this information to you, Saul, that Dr. Ludwig Stumfegger was found right beside the man whom we think is Martin Bormann. You should know that these two men were seen earlier by eyewitnesses together in nineteen forty-five."

"I am aware of that fact," I said knowingly.

"Very well," he said. "This person," Klopfer said as he pointed to Dr. Stumfegger, "is definitely the doctor, okay? So, we do not need to review this information."

"Fine," I agreed.

"Okay, this first report is by the Land Institute for Forensic and Social Medicine done on the skeleton. The one believed to be Martin Bormann had a body height of one hundred sixty-eight to one hundred seventy-two centimeters and a head circumference of fifty-five to fifty-seven centimeters. The skull is round. The body height of one hundred seventy centimeters fits the data given us by the SS Register of Prominent Members.

"According to extensive X-ray examination, this revealed a defective knit which may be seen following a fracture of the right collarbone. The information agrees with Bormann's son's story that his father had a broken collarbone as a result of an accident he had while riding a horse in 1938 or 1939.

"The teeth were next to be examined. This was done by the Police Dental Clinic in Berlin on January fourth, nineteen eighty-three. The comparison was done with a dental chart by Dr. Blaschke, who worked on Bormann's teeth for over ten years. Their conclusion was that the dental work in the skull was done by Dr. Blaschke and is highly suggestive of the chart which belongs to Martin Bormann.

"The fourth test, and probably one of the most interesting, was done by the state prosecutors of the Supreme District Court of Frankfurt-on-Main who commissioned the Chief Pathologist to reconstruct the face from the basis of the skull that existed."

"Very interesting," I added. I was just taking in about half of what Herr Klopfer was telling me, but I tried to appear interested anyway.

"Listen to this, Saul. In order to have objectivity, the test was supervised, and several skulls were modeled. The Chief Pathologist was not given access to any Document Center papers on Stumfegger or Bormann.

"Anyway, both faces were done very carefully for detail and artistic excellence. The comparison cross-check with pictures taken of Bormann in nineteen forty-five shows unequivocally that the skull is that of Martin Bormann."

Klopfer sat down in his chair and leaned back, putting his feet on his desk blotter. A smug look came across his face.

"Well, Saul, it will take a lot of convincing to substantiate your side of this tale."

I looked at Herr Klopfer, turned, and then walked slowly over to a chair perched in front of his desk. How could I tell my side of this story convincingly enough to jar some action from this office?

"Herr Klopfer, I think that you are a man who deals with the truth, and what I am about to divulge to you has to be kept in the strictest confidence or it could mean somebody's life."

I looked straight into his eyes and stared to add more suspense to my story.

"One day last year, I received a phone call from a fellow agent of mine, by the name of Herman Kreisberg. Does that ring a bell, Klopfer?" I questioned.

"Ah, no, I haven't heard of the name," he responded.

"Oh, I thought you might have. He is one of our top men out of Haifa, Israel. Anyway, to continue, he called me last year and was very distressed about something. It seemed that one night while in a bar in Asuncion, Paraguay, Herman and another agent named Sidney Rubenstein ran into a doctor who was nearly drunk. As the three men began to talk, the doctor divulged that he had treated Martin Bormann for a duodenal ulcer in a jungle villa somewhere on the Parana River, north of Paraguay."

Herr Klopfer looked doubtful, but I continued anyway.

"To make a long story short, my man, Sidney found the so-called villa and overheard a conversation between a man who resembled Bormann and someone else who was unknown to him. Sidney told

Herman that he had overheard the two men talking about a German agent and scientist who went to the Russians after World War II and eventually worked his way up in the Russian Nuclear Weapons Program. His plan was to fake a nuclear attack on the United States, and in the process, provoke a U.S. attack on Russia."

"How would this benefit Bormann?" Klopfer replied sarcastically, putting his hands behind his head.

"It's simple," I stressed, "the United States was already at the breaking point with Russia. After the two countries and their allies had annihilated themselves, then Bormann, who has a very advanced and well-financed colony in South America, could infiltrate right back here to start the Fourth Reich ... and that is what scares me."

"What's that, Simon?"

"Herr Klopfer," I said in a disgusted manner, "the Nuclear War has already happened. Suppose this story is really true."

Suddenly the office door opened, and a balding man walked in.

"Adolf," Klopfer said in a friendly way. "What a pleasant surprise," he added as he jumped out of his chair and walked over to greet him.

"Sit down, Alfred. No need to get up on my account," he responded.

They shook hands.

"Oh, Adolf ... I have a man here I would like you to meet."

The man turned to me as I got out of my chair to greet him.

"Adolf, this is Saul Weinberg of the Jewish Liberation League. Saul, I would like you to meet Adolf Stolz, the man about whom we were talking in relation to Karl Frahm's accident."

As we shook hands, I looked at Klopfer questioningly.

"You remember, Saul. Adolf is the person from the Reichstag Security Office who verified that Karl Frahm's car had been already dented in the parking lot prior to his accident."

"Oh, that's right, silly of me to have forgotten."

I looked at Stolz, trying to study him discreetly. I just had a gut feeling there was more to him than met the eye. For some curious reason I had the strange feeling that I knew this man from some other place. I thought back. Maybe I had met him while living in Munich with Simon after World War II. I always hated this feeling, when I had something or somebody on the edge of my mind, but could not quite remember. He wasn't even a friendly man. I could never trust a person who wouldn't even have the courtesy to smile when he met someone.

"What brings Weinberg all the way from Israel?" Stolz questioned suspiciously.

A smile came to Klopfer's face.

"It seems Herr Weinberg has a story which proves that Martin Bormann is still alive and well."

I could not believe what I was hearing. He was divulging the information to a stranger. I tried to interrupt him but was cut off by Klopfer.

"He also believes that somehow Bormann had something to do with the Nuclear War starting and is going to lead the Nazi party in Germany again."

I exploded.

"That is not what I said, Klopfer, and besides I told you this information was only between you and me!"

I paced the floor nervously.

"Weinberg," Klopfer said. "Don't worry. Adolf is from the Security Office. If we cannot trust him, then we cannot trust anyone. He deals with me in many cases and is always well informed of my investigations."

The two looked at each other with smirks on their faces. Stolz interjected.

"Herr Weinberg, the evidence we have on Bormann is conclusive and leaves no doubt that he is very dead indeed."

"So Herr Klopfer has told me, and told me, and told me. I would rather not discuss the issue any further with you, if you don't mind," I answered sternly.

Klopfer interrupted and tried to change the subject to avoid a verbal confrontation between Stolz and me.

"What brings you to this part of the building, Adolf?" he asked politely.

He glanced toward Klopfer.

"It seems that I lost my wallet some time yesterday, Alfred, and before you arrived yesterday I had to pull a file down here. Have you seen it at all?"

"No, I haven't," he answered.

My eyes began to scan the room frantically, trying to locate the wallet. If I could find it, maybe it would supply me with some valuable information.

Suddenly I spotted it behind the leg of a chair located beside the filing cabinet. This was my big chance. I walked over and sat down in the chair and in a nonchalant manner picked up a magazine and began flipping through the pages, hoping the two men would think I was just killing time until they had taken care of their business.

As they proceeded to check around the filing cabinet, I carefully put my foot on top of the wallet to hide it from their view. Then they made their way over to the desk to investigate further. When they had their backs turned to me, I swiftly bent down and picked up the wallet. I tucked it neatly into the inside pocket of my blazer and breathed a sigh of relief.

Adolf, not finding his wallet, left, and I continued my story to Alfred. Needless to say, Klopfer was not much help at all, dismissing the pertinent information I divulged to him as unsubstantiated and vague. He wished me a good day in his best bureaucratic voice. I was not unduly concerned because I was anxious to get home and examine the contents of Stolz's wallet, hoping it would give Simon and I another clue to further our investigation.

## Chapter 9

The blue velvet couch creaked sharply as Bormann sat back to comfort himself. In the background he could hear a high-pitched whistle which signaled that his coffee was ready. He made an effort to get up from the couch, but Rudi jumped out of his seat and quickly walked into the kitchen to fetch the kettle.

"Father," he spoke sternly, "you are going to have to learn to relax. This constant running around is bad for you."

Rudi stood there looking upset.

"Ah, Rudi, you baby me too much," Bormann responded. "In fact, you have nothing to worry about. I am in very good health as you well know."

"I know, Father, but please just take it easy," he pleaded. "Okay?"

"All right," Bormann chuckled.

Rudi approached his father with a large mug of hot coffee and handed it to him. Then he returned to his seat.

"Thank you, Rudi. You are a gracious host."

Bormann blew on the coffee to cool it down, and then sipped it carefully. It tasted very good. He relaxed and leaned back in his seat.

"Now, Rudi, continue with what you were saying."

"Well, Father, from the details that you have told me about the way you ran the Fuhrer's affairs, I just don't know if I can handle it as smoothly as you did. You are ..."

"Rudi," Bormann interrupted. "You must have confidence as a leader and as a good orator. There is one thing I was never good at and that was making a speech. You are versed in all aspects of public life and should exceed my level of success."

"But, Father," he pleaded. "You seemed to know with whom to speak and who to impress in order to get ahead in government."

"The thing you want, Rudi, is to eventually separate from the conventional government offices and to have your own inner circle of men who will do as you tell them. The only way I could achieve my success was to never be the hero of a dramatic scene and to never be in the limelight. This is not what you have been taught. Your road to success will take a different route."

"But the members of the old party system seem destined to have their own way. Every time I get close to more additional legislation to help our cause, the party members bind together to help override it."

"Rudi, Rudi," Bormann said calmly. "The only way to find success in this type of situation is to play one person against the other. If the people who oppose you turn on each other, you will eventually be the person with the leverage.

"I also had another tool which I used to hurt party functionaries. His name was Reinhard Heydrich, a very crafty character. He had been dismissed from the Navy at one time, only to become Chief of the Security Service and the Security Police. He was vested with both government and SS authority which made him a most useful tool. In fact, his office was located at Berlin Gestapo Headquarters on Prinz Albrecht Strasse, not far from his house.

"Heydrich had access to government files on every political leader, which made him quite an unpopular man. He also obtained much damaging information about political members and kept an accurate record on all these members' vices and wrongdoings.

"I became very good friends with Heydrich only to obtain this needed information to keep the party members on their toes. But as always, Heydrich kept trying to expand his powers, which made me very nervous.

"At one time, he had been in line for a promotion to take control of Bohemia and Moravia. The top party members of course suggested Heydrich as a good possibility. I told the Fuhrer that he was not responsible enough to handle such a post. He did, however, win control of the two provinces. I did everything in my power to keep him away from the Fuhrer and eventually Hitler became uninterested in him."

"But Father," Rudi interrupted. "Who can you trust in this kind of situation?"

"The only person you can trust while moving up the political ladder is yourself," he said. "Look at the men closest to Hitler. They all became greedy and thought only of themselves instead of the Third Reich.

"Hermann Goering, for instance, a highly decorated pilot and Hitler's hand-picked successor, became a lover of luxury and drugs. Daily he consumed one hundred tablets of Paracodeine. He eventually cared only about his fabulous art collection which had been looted from every part of Europe.

"Another close ally of the Fuhrer's was Joseph Goebbels. He was a brilliant man who had acquired a Ph.D. in Philosophy from the University of Heidelberg. As a member of the Nazi Party in nineteen twenty-five, he was the first person who understood how to control the minds of the masses through propaganda techniques such as radio, films, the press, loudspeakers, and even posters. He became unpopular with Hitler because, even though he was highly intelligent, he was cynical. Also, he was a married man with six children but established liaisons with many young actresses.

"One of Hitler's closest friends, and my arch rival, was Heinrich Himmler. He was originally a poultry farmer from outside Munich.

Eventually, he was appointed Reich Fuhrer of the SS. He acquired immense power, controlling all police agencies from the Gestapo to the Regular Order Police. Himmler was not a particularly smart man, but I respected him because he did carry out Hitler's racial policy against the Jews. However, he too ran into difficulty. The man was scrupulously honest with money, but here his sense of honesty ended. Himmler became involved with his secretary and she bore him a son. He was already married and financially the situation became a burden for him to carry. He was forced to borrow eighty thousand marks out of Party funds. He also let the Fuhrer down while commanding an army group guarding the advance by the Russians across the Oder River near Frankfurt.

"Probably the closest person to the Fuhrer, and the biggest traitor of all, was Rudolf Hess. He joined the Nazi party as its sixteenth member. Hess eventually ended up in jail with the Fuhrer at Landsberg Prison as a result of a fight at a Munich brewery. In prison, Hess took dictation for the book *Mein Kampf*. The bonds between Hitler and Hess appeared to be unbreakable.

"I'll never forget that Sunday morning when my brother, Albert, broke into the daily report session and dropped a letter from Hess into the Fuhrer's hand. The Fuhrer just said, 'Oh, my God! He's gone to England.' It turned out that Rudolf Hess had stolen a Messerschmitt 110 plane and added two seven-hundred-liter petrol tanks to take him to England. Hess apparently wanted to try to help secure an alliance between Germany and England. The Fuhrer said he had broken under the immense strain of his party position.

"People affiliated with Hess were arrested. All photographs of Hess, and books and official literature bearing his pictures, were destroyed. This affair tore the guts out of the Fuhrer and that is when I made up my mind that no one in government can be trusted."

Rudi rose from his seat and walked over to the window. He looked up and down the street.

"Father," he said in a passive manner, "I hope everything goes the way you have planned. I would hate to let you down."

Bormann got up from the couch and walked over to Rudi.

"Son, never second guess yourself," Bormann began, patting him on the shoulder. "You have been everything I have hoped and planned for. Inside my heart the feeling grows stronger every day that our mission will succeed, and the Fourth Reich will overcome triumphantly."

Suddenly, Bormann heard a pounding on the front door. The sound was intense. Rudi hurried across the blue Oriental carpet to answer the door. As he opened it, Bormann noticed Adolf Stolz standing there, perspiring heavily. He was panting as well.

"Adolf, how are you?" Rudi asked warmly.

"We have a tremendous problem," he responded nervously, walking in and shedding his brown suit jacket.

Bormann turned and walked over to confer with him. "Adolf, what has happened?" he asked, his heart beginning to race spasmodically.

"Well, Martin. A man visited Alfred Klopfer's office today from Haifa, Israel. His name is Saul Weinberg, a Nazi hunter."

"That is not so unusual, Adolf. Many men visit that office from time to time."

"But this man knows that you are alive. He also knows that we were responsible for the Nuclear War last year and that we are attempting to control the government and to reenact Nazi ideologies."

Bormann exploded furiously, "How could he know such a thing? This can't be true!"

Adolf walked toward Bormann.

"Sir, the only way Saul Weinberg could have obtained this information is if he received it from that spy we killed last year. Remember, he was found on the terrace observing you. He had a two-way radio on his person and perhaps before he died, he managed to relay a message back to his people."

"Adolf, how many other people might possibly have this same knowledge?" Bormann asked harshly.

"I'm not sure, Sir. We really don't have any way of knowing."

Rudi interrupted, "Adolf, did this man leave an address where he could be reached?"

"Herr Klopfer said he was staying at Eislon Strasse Number Fourteen, which is two kilometers south of here. This man sounds like trouble, Sir. If he keeps snooping around, then he might reveal some very damaging information to the police, or even worse."

"Well, what do you suggest, Adolf?"

Bormann stood there with his arms crossed, waiting for an answer.

"Martin, this situation has to be dealt with immediately. We must insure that Weinberg communicates with no one else. I suggest disposing of everyone at the household and hope this incident does not become a thorn in our sides."

Adolf stood there, awaiting another outburst from Bormann, but one did not come. Bormann could feel his stomach becoming upset and he began to ache in the abdominal region. He walked across the floor to the couch clutching his stomach and trying to hold back all the pain coming from within. He fell on the couch, hoping that the pain would diminish. As he lay there, his mind journeyed back to the afternoon of April twenty-second, nineteen forty-five, in the bunker under the Reich chancellery.

It seemed that with every passing hour, Hitler had become increasingly more upset. Berlin was literally being surrounded by the Allies and would soon be cut off from the rest of the country. After the report that Steiner's attack to relieve Berlin was still being organized, Hitler ordered everyone out of the conference room except Bormann and his generals. Suddenly, he lunged to his feet, yelling that he was encircled by traitors who did not understand his great purpose. Bormann had never seen the Fuhrer become so upset before. He said to himself then that he would never let his thoughts be clouded by such outbursts.

"Father, Father, are you all right?" Rudi asked with concern.

He ran to a nearby cabinet and snatched his bottle of ulcer medication. With shaking hands, Rudi took one pill from the bottle and placed it in his father's palm. Adolf came up behind Rudi with a small glass of milk to help his ailing stomach. Bormann gulped down the milk and the pill and sat back, laying his head on the armrest.

"I'll be all right, Rudi. Don't worry yourself," Bormann consoled. "This news has upset you."

Rudi turned to Adolf, who was sitting in a brown rocking chair.

"Well, is this mess going to be cleared up, Adolf? You know what we are up against," he snapped.

"Don't worry, Rudi," Stoltz said confidently. "The situation will be remedied at once, Sir."

As Bormann lay on the couch, he could hear a squeak coming from the rocking chair. He could only hope that these enemies of the Reich did not bring any comrades to help aid them.

When we finally take over the government, he thought, these Jews and all other Jews will be dealt with appropriately.

## Chapter 10

25 July 1985

I could feel a gentle east wind blowing as we brought the boat around to a starboard tack. My arm was fully extended on the tiller to bring the boat into the wind. We had been fanning for quite some time now and I wanted to impress Judith with my boating skills. It was a beautiful day, just perfect for outdoor activity. The Wannsee Recreational Area was a popular spot for boating and swimming in Berlin, but even with the crowds, it was still quite relaxing. Judith often came out here to go sailing and to get away from her responsibilities at the museum.

It seemed a shame that Simon could not have accompanied us to the lake today. Herr Schmidt had come to rely on our help in the bakery, and with business being heavy on Saturday, it was just as well that he stayed there to help.

The past two days Simon and I had spent examining Adolf Stolz's wallet very carefully. I was positive that this would give us a lead to more crucial information, but going over its contents with a fine-tooth comb had revealed nothing out of the ordinary.

The wallet contained forty marks, many family photographs, a driver's license, Security ID, and several credit cards. Simon said he would keep reviewing its contents hoping some kind of clue would arise.

As I looked up to the mast, I noticed the mainsheet was starting to luff very loudly. Using a last resort, I jerked the tiller sharply, trying to bring the boat about, but it was no use.

Judith woke up out of a sound sleep in my lap, sitting up beside me.

"What is the matter, Saul? Didn't you remember all my instructions?" she asked, laughingly.

I sat there somewhat embarrassed about my lack of boating skills.

"Well, I just cannot seem to get the hang of this. It's a good thing I'm not out at sea by myself."

Judith chuckled, "You wouldn't mind if we both got marooned on a desert island with no one to save us, would you?"

"Wow!" I said, "Now that would be a dream come true."

Judith reached over and gave me a kiss on the cheek. I put my arms around her to bring her closer.

"Now, Saul," she scolded, "first things first. Let's get this boat back on course."

She slid over to grab the tiller and moved it ever so slightly toward us. The main sheet began to fill up with wind and the boat tilted just a bit. I put my hand on the edge to hold on. The boom moved away from us slowly and Judith locked the rope into the jib cleat. Immediately we started increasing in speed.

"That was great," I complimented.

"It's not so hard, Saul, if you practice as much as I do," she said, looking over at me and smiling. "Now we have time for more important business." Judith put her arms around my neck and began kissing me passionately. She was very sure of herself and this was a trait I admired.

I put my hands up on the sides of her breasts and began reciprocating with affection. We slid down into the cockpit of the boat, embracing. How I wished that life could only be this simple and lovely.

After a few windswept minutes, Judith nestled her head upon my chest to relax. We sat there, completely at ease, as the boat jetted through the water. I looked and noticed Judith's eyes were closed so I decided to do the same.

"Saul," Judith said, startling me.

"Yeah," I responded.

"What are you thinking about?" she questioned.

"Are you sure you really want to know?"

"Yes, of course," she said.

"Well, I was thinking about Mr. Adolf Stolz," I admitted. "I can't seem to get him out of my mind."

"Is that the man whose wallet you found?" Judith asked.

"Yes, it is. He seems so familiar to me, but I just cannot place where I may have run across him before."

I sat back, shaking my head.

"Well, Saul, maybe he just reminds you of someone you met before. It happens to people all the time," she consoled, patting me on the shoulder.

"I just know I have met him or seen him before. The weird thing about this is that he generates an atmosphere of evil. I could feel it when he walked into the office."

I tried to concentrate. Stolz, where had I heard this name before? Stolz ... Stolz ....

"Oh no, oh no," I muttered.

"What's the matter?" Judith asked, looking very concerned.

"His name is Alfred Stolz, not Adolf," I said in an anxious manner. "Oh, my God, now I remember." My heart began to race.

"Remember what?" Judith was tapping me on the shoulder.

"This man I met the other day was a tank commander in the Waffen SS near Russia in nineteen forty-one."

"How can you be sure, Saul?" Judith questioned. "It was so long ago."

"I know he is the same man. He is an animal. He was responsible for the deaths of at least one thousand people in the Balkans. How could I forget someone like him?" I asked abruptly.

"Are you sure, Saul? Are you absolutely sure?"

"Yes, I am sure. I can remember the case like it was yesterday. One day when we were working at the Documentation Center in Vienna, a little old lady came hobbling in and sat down beside my desk. She was a Russian Jew from the village of Mizocz in the Volyn near the town of Kovel, not far from the Russian border. Her story described a German Waffen SS tank column on its way east toward the Russian front for a secret spring offensive. The German soldiers had gone from house to house, rounding up every living person they could find. The lady said she hid beneath some false floorboards and avoided being captured.

After the soldiers and townspeople had left, she crept up to the second floor of her home to view the situation outside. As she peered out the window, she saw several hundred people being ushered into a small ravine. The German soldiers surrounded the ravine and began firing their machine guns down into it. The lady began to break down and cry in my arms, saying she would never be able to forget the screams and the horror of it all. Two soldiers entered the house to seize the owners. As they searched from room to room, she heard the name Alfred Stolz mentioned as their leader."

Judith looked up at me with tears pouring down her cheeks. She reached over, popped the rope out of the jib cleat and let the main sheet all the way out. The boat began to catch the wind and tip up on end just a bit. I anticipated we were returning to the boat rental dock.

My ignorance of Judith's feelings had upset her very much. But even with the harshness of past realities, I figured she was better off knowing the truth.

# The Descendant

********

My hands were perspiring on the steering wheel of Judith's Volkswagen as we raced back toward town. I was nervously anticipating Simon's reaction to my verification of Alfred Stolz's identity. Judith sat quietly on the passenger side of the car, glancing out the window at the passing scenery. A thousand thoughts kept entering my mind as to how our investigation would go from here. The only positive way to verify the truth would be to compare Alfred Stolz's driver's license with the picture of him in the documentation file.

As I turned the corner down Eislon Strasse, I saw a mass of fire equipment and firefighters battling an inferno coming from the bakery.

Judith screamed, "Oh my God, Saul, what's happened?"

I pulled the car over quickly and bolted out toward the fire. As I ran closer, a policeman grabbed me by the arm.

"Halt," the man said.

I tried to tear myself free.

"I live here, don't you understand?"

"What is your name?" the policeman demanded. "Saul, Saul Weinberg."

"Come with me, then."

The man led me over to a rescue truck parked across the street from the burning bakery. He opened the door and I stepped up and in. Two paramedics were working on a badly burned man. As I looked closer, I was horrified and shocked.

"Simon, Simon," I put my fist into my mouth and bit down hard. "Oh my God! Simon!"

One of the paramedics looked over.

"Is your name Saul?" he asked. "Yes, it is," I said in a low voice.

"He has been muttering your name for the past few minutes," the paramedic said.

"What happened? How did the fire start?" I asked anxiously.

The other man stood up and walked over.

"The only thing we know right now is that a green Mercedes pulled up in front of the bakery and someone inside it flung some sort of explosive through the front window."

"How is Simon? Will he make it?"

Both men gave me a discomforting look.

"He's burned very badly," one said. "Over ninety percent of his body."

Then I heard a voice moaning, calling my name. I looked over at Simon. He was moving ever so slightly.

The paramedic looked up at me.

"Why don't you see if you can comfort him," he suggested.

I bent down and knelt at Simon's side. His face was almost unrecognizable. A chilling feeling came over me as I grasped his hand.

I whispered in his ear, "Simon, it's Saul. It's all right. I am here to take care of you."

Simon turned his head slowly looking into my eyes.

He cleared his throat, coughing spasmodically. "Saul," he whispered.

I knelt closer to hear him. He forced out a short sentence in broken Yiddish, smiled, and then his eyes rolled up slowly into his head. I cupped my hands over his face, closing his eyelids.

"What did he say?" one of the paramedics asked. I looked up at him.

"He said, 'Obtain justice for the six million.'"

Both men looked at each other with puzzled looks on their faces.

At that moment, the back door of the ambulance opened. Judith appeared with a policeman comforting her. I rushed over to the back of the ambulance to stop her from viewing Simon.

"Saul," she cried uncontrollably, "the Schmidts are both dead."

Her crying was muffled as she buried her face into the policeman's shoulder.

The sorrow in my heart was quickly being overcome by a fit of anger and hatred. The time had come for the guilty to be punished. I looked up at the policeman and said, with mixed emotions, "Take care of her."

I ran over to Judith's car, jumped in and took off, not really knowing what I was going to do. After I had driven only a few blocks, I remembered that a copy of Alfred Stolz's address was in the glove compartment of the car. My hands were moist with perspiration as I turned the switch to open the compartment. After a few seconds of rummaging, I pulled out a small piece of paper with the name Adolf Stolz and the address, thirty-six Herder Strasse, Berlin, Germany, written on it. Here in my hands was the only lead as to the murderers of Simon and the Schmidts.

Again, I reached into the compartment and pulled out a local map of the Berlin area, locating Herder Strasse.

"Great," I said to myself. "Only a little over a kilometer from here."

I dropped the map onto the passenger seat and drove on. My mind was racing. How would I approach the situation? My only advantage at this time was my intense hatred of the people with whom I would have to deal. The short drive seemed to take forever.

There it was, Herder Strasse. I took a quick right-hand turn, and as I pulled up in front of the Swiss-designed building, I began scanning for number thirty-six. I hoped to see a green Mercedes around, but there were none in sight.

Then I removed my revolver from the leather holster strapped under my arm and examined it to make damn sure it was in working order. I took a few deep breaths, and stepped out of the car.

Once inside the front door, I read down the list of tenants until I came to the name Stolz. Ah, there it was, Adolf Stolz, apartment number 45.

I turned the corner, deciding to take the elevator instead of the stairs. After pushing the up button, I heard the quiet sound of an electric motor lowering the elevator. As the elevator doors opened, I got a nervous feeling that an enemy would spring from the carrier. I reached quickly for my gun but when the door opened, the elevator was empty. A feeling of relief came over me as I pressed the button for the fourth floor.

The elevator doors slammed shut as the car rose slowly to its destination. I looked up at the floor numbers displayed above the doors and saw number three light up. All of a sudden, the car jerked to a halt.

What could be wrong? I wondered. Calmly, I pushed the fourth-floor button, but there was no response. I was just about to push the alarm button when I heard a noise from the top of the car. Glancing up through the false ceiling, I noticed the escape hatch was slightly ajar.

Just then a white pellet, the size of an olive, dropped to the floor of the car throwing off a thin layer of white vapor.

"Oh my God!" I shouted.

My first thought was that it was poisonous gas. Was this the end? Would I die like my parents in the gas chambers of Auschwitz? I went to pull my gun but elected to take out a handkerchief to cover my mouth instead. It was time for split-second thinking. With one hand, I reached up and grabbed the false ceiling, ripping it down onto the floor. Taking one last breath of air from my handkerchief, I sprang up to the top of the car, popping the hatch off.

With every last bit of strength in my arms, I pulled my body to freedom. As I lay on the top of the car catching my breath, I noticed that the elevator doors on the fourth floor were opened just a bit.

After resting a few moments to regain my strength, I reached up and grabbed a long steel beam mounted on the elevator shaft. I tried to cat walk my way to safety, but my sweaty hands were making it extremely difficult.

As I grunted and groaned my way to the exit, I felt increasingly vulnerable. Someone might intercept me at the fourth-floor opening. It was a chance I would have to take.

I finally grabbed the elevator doors on the fourth floor, pulling my body up onto the floor as a seal would. Removing my gun, I could feel it sliding around in my hands.

The hallway was completely deserted. I covered my eyes to shield them from the strong glare of the sun beaming in from a window at the end of the hall. I then pushed myself up to my feet as I crept like a cat toward apartment number 45.

The time had finally come. There it was staring me in the face. What was on the other side of that big brown door? It could be the revenge I had long awaited, or just the death of another Jew. My heart was beating rapidly.

I backed off about a foot from the entrance, then threw a flying kick, splintering the door as it opened. Using my gun as the point man, I stuck my head in through the door.

To my surprise I heard a strong voice from within say, "Come in, Mr. Weinberg. I've been expecting you."

An old man was sitting on the other side of the room in a brown rocking chair. How did he know my name? My heart began to race at a fantastic speed. Oh, my God, I thought to myself. This man rocking back and forth in his chair had a very strong likeness to the diabolical Martin Bormann.

Had I really found him? Could I have walked in on the headquarters of his fiendish scheme?

An atmosphere of doom settled over me. I quickly turned my head to check the hallway. It was too late. A blow hit the back of my neck and everything went black.

********

My sight was blurry, and my eyes opened to see the same man seated across from me. A sharp pain raced up the back of my neck into my head. To my surprise, my hands were free to soothe the ache that was increasing by the minute. I was amazed that I was still alive, since the gas pellet in the elevator indicated that my assailants meant business.

As my eyes focused more clearly, I finally recognized that the man in the rocking chair was indeed Hitler's right-hand man, Martin Bormann. He was very old but seemed to be in good condition for a man his age. His head was bald except for a trace of hair on the sides, and he seemed to be several pounds overweight. His blue eyes seemed to stare right through me, making me increasingly uneasy.

I was tempted to make a move to overpower him, since he was unarmed, but as my head turned to the right, I noticed another man standing by the door with a luger pointed right at my head. The man, fitted in a smart-looking, tailored, brown three-piece suit, was extremely large with broad shoulders.

From the look on his face, I decided to sit very still until I could think of my next move.

"So, Mr. Weinberg, we finally meet," Bormann said in a self-assured voice, glancing over at the other man for his reaction. "We decided that if you were a good enough detective to have pieced our mission together, it would only be a matter of time until you would find our apartment. Isn't that true, Mr. Weinberg?"

"It was no problem at all with Adolf Stolz's driver's license and identification cards," I said conceitedly.

"By the way, where did you leave Stolz's wallet?" Bormann questioned.

"It burned in the fire at the bakery, just like my friend Simon and the Schmidt family did, you bastard!" My voice had become very loud and piercing.

"Come, come, Mr. Weinberg. You should well know that the bomb was meant for you and your partner. The two of you are responsible for the deaths of the Schmidts by staying at their home. But nevertheless, what is done is done." Bormann sat there tapping one of his fingers on the arm of the rocking chair.

"Mr. Weinberg," he spoke respectfully, "the reason Hans and I have let you locate us is that we were impressed with the way you trailed us to Berlin. Before we exterminate you, we wanted you to know exactly what you would have eventually uncovered yourself."

My stomach dropped when Bormann said the word "exterminate." It was a word I had heard many times before and it still made me uncomfortable to hear it now.

"You won't get away with this charade, Bormann," I said sternly. "Many people already know of your intentions."

Bormann began to chuckle in a chilling tone. "Come now, Mr. Weinberg, you have no more friends to help you. We have an adequate intelligence network to know this. Why don't you just admit that you are defeated at your own game?"

"Don't worry, my friends will follow your trail long after I am dead and gone," I reiterated.

Bormann got up out of the brown rocking chair and removed a framed picture from the mantel over the fireplace. It was of a man in his early forties with black hair, wearing a brown suit. He walked only a few steps and flung the picture toward my face. With a reflex action, I raised my hands quickly to catch the picture.

"Do you know who this man is, Mr. Weinberg?" he questioned.

I glanced over to the other man for a reaction. He had a big grin on his face.

"No," I answered abruptly. "I have never seen this man before."

"I am surprised you have not, Weinberg, since you are supposed to be such a great detective," Bormann said sarcastically. "Well for your information, his name is Rudolf Hitler. He is the illegitimate son of Adolf Hitler and will lead the Fourth Reich to the world domination of the Aryan race. Does this surprise you, Mr. Weinberg?" he asked.

I was speechless. How could such a thing be true? Could these beasts have pulled off such a loathsome mission?

"That's impossible," I responded. "Such a thing could not be true."

"That's where you are wrong, Mr. Weinberg. Rudolf Hitler is a reality and is a well-respected member of the provisionary government at the Reichstag. He is also well versed in Nazi ideologies and has the potential to lead Germany when the time is right. So, Mr. Weinberg, you have failed, and all your Jewish assassins will not have the final victory."

Bormann sat there with a smug look on his face. My stomach had a sinking, queasy feeling. I must stall for time to think of an escape route, I thought. Keep Bormann talking, that's it—the only way.

"Was this rebirth of the Nazi regime planned, Herr Bormann?" I asked.

"Of course it was, you fool. The German people are a very organized race," he scolded. "It was unfortunate for all loyal Germans that the Fuhrer's health was breaking down. It's funny ... I remember so well. It was the beginning of May, nineteen forty-four, when the Fuhrer was restricted to bed with a bad headache. We were concerned at the time and decided to bring in Dr. Erwin Giesing, a faithful and trusted physician.

"When he entered the Fuhrer's bedroom, the Fuhrer was lying in bed, so he went to his bedside to greet him. The Fuhrer was so weak that his head fell back to the pillow. His eyes were empty, almost lifeless, and his skin had a yellow tinge suggesting jaundice.

"Dr. Giesing revealed that the Fuhrer's medication he had been prescribed for intestinal cramps was a combination of strychnine and atropine. If taken incorrectly these were two deadly poisons. Dr. Giesing questioned the Fuhrer as to the physician who had prescribed such treatment, but the Fuhrer brushed Giesing off, saying that he felt better after taking his pills. I decided to suggest that the doctor give the Fuhrer a complete examination, to insure he was physically fine. He agreed enthusiastically.

"The doctor started his series of simple tests and, as time went on, the doctor's facial expression became serious. I knew something was drastically wrong with the Fuhrer. After the doctor had finished his examination, he assured the Fuhrer that he was in good health and bade him farewell.

"As we walked out of the bedroom, the doctor asked to talk with me alone in my office. Once there, he informed me of the fact that the Fuhrer had symptoms of Parkinson's disease, characterized by trembling of the limbs and rigidity of certain muscles. He knew from previous tests that the Fuhrer also suffered from anxiety, nervous depression, and frequent hysterical outbursts, which specifically narrowed the diagnosis.

"I could not believe what I was hearing. The final straw was that no therapy was known, and the condition would worsen and jeopardize the Fuhrer's decision-making abilities.

"The good doctor was paid ten thousand marks to keep the diagnosis a secret and prevent panic among the heads of staff, or even worse, the German people."

"It seems quite fair," I laughed.

"What's fair?" Bormann barked at me.

"Only that a man who was responsible for so much violence and suffering have such an unpleasant ending of his own life." I laughed again just to infuriate Bormann.

He sat there expressionless, and then gave a hand signal to the man at the door. I knew that I had gone too far. The man proceeded to come over and hit me in the face with his gun. A sharp pain raced up the side of my face as I yelled.

Now it was Bormann's turn to laugh.

"Mr. Weinberg, you should have more respect for such a great man and a devoted leader."

I was thinking of several snide remarks to throw at him, but decided to keep my mouth shut to save my jawbone.

"Come now, Mr. Weinberg, there is more to the story than that," he said. "But if we have another remark like that one, you probably won't live to hear the end."

A contented smile came to Bormann's face as he sat back in the rocking chair. He continued with his bizarre story.

"After the shock of Dr. Giesing's diagnosis had worn off, I realized that we had to plan for the continuation, or the rebirth, of the Thousand Year Reich if by chance it crumbled. I immediately sent for Heinrich Himmler to confer on such a delicate matter, even though my personal views on the man were very low.

"After I explained the situation to him, he suggested that the Fuhrer be blessed with some offspring to carry on the leadership of the Nazi regime. My first thoughts were how could we keep such a thing a secret?

"Himmler enlightened me to the fact that he had supplied many young and beautiful Frauleins to the Fuhrer for his sexual pleasures. Up until that time, the unfortunate ones who had become pregnant were whisked off to Himmler's unofficial headquarters in Hohenlychen some seventy-five miles north of Berlin. There they were murdered, and all official records of their existence were destroyed. The Fuhrer was always kept in the dark as to their disappearances.

"Himmler and I decided that the next girl to become impregnated by the Fuhrer would be chosen to donate her offspring for the leadership of the German people and the glory of the Third Reich.

"After several girls had been entertained by the Fuhrer, a

housekeeper by the name of Geli Reiter came to me in tears with the news that she had slept with the Fuhrer several times and had become pregnant. She was a beautiful young fraulein with long blonde hair, soft skin, and a figure that would warm any man's blood.

"Our job turned out to be easier than we thought. She claimed that she was unworthy to have the Fuhrer's child and wanted to know if I could arrange an abortion. I consoled her and told her I knew a doctor in Hohenlychen that could abort the baby. She agreed and was turned over to Himmler.

"I never saw the fraulein again but in February of the next year, I received a phone call from Himmler verifying that the fraulein had given birth to a handsome baby boy.

"The rest was easy, Mr. Weinberg. After things started falling apart in Berlin, we planned our escape to Brazil by boat where the gears of Nazism were already in motion. We were a well-financed group having ..."

I began to think to myself as Bormann continued. How could I get to the man by the door without getting shot? My plan had to go into motion soon or I would be dead. Well, I really had nothing to lose anyway; besides, Bormann was unarmed and too old to defend himself.

I figured the goon by the door was about fifteen feet away. Somehow, I would have to distract him for a split second.

Then it came to me. I reached slowly into my right pocket and removed a silver coin I had on me. My hands were perspiring heavily. I had to regrip the coin to avoid dropping it. As Bormann continued his little story, I dropped my arm down the side of the chair and with a flick of my wrist, rolled the coin under my chair across the room. As it hit the opposite wall, the guard turned away from me to see what the noise was.

I lunged from my seat, grabbing a flower pot on a nearby

bookshelf. With split-second timing, I hurled the pot at the man's trigger hand, knocking the gun to the floor.

There was my break. I used my body as a weapon at the man's midsection and landed a kick in his groin. He slumped over for a moment in agony.

As I grabbed for the gun on the floor, he landed a crushing blow with his foot to my hand. The pain rushed immediately up my arm but the adrenaline running through my body dulled the pain quickly.

All of a sudden, he kicked me in the face, throwing me backward. The gun was hooked around one of my fingers as I landed on the floor. He was on me immediately, with a fierce, killer look in his eyes. His hands were forcing the gun around in my direction.

I used all the strength I had just to stall the movement of the gun.

Suddenly there was a shot, throwing the man back onto the floor. There he lay, not moving. I wheeled around to end Martin Bormann's life, but instead, stood looking down the barrel of another gun, held by Bormann who wore a sick smile.

Just as I focused in on the weapon, there was a flash, and then a following jolt hit me in the face. As I fell back to the floor, I knew the end had arrived.

## Chapter 11

Karl Dieter made his way slowly down the street towards his favorite bakery. He left his apartment as quietly as possible to not wake his wife. She always loved to sleep in since they retired, and he never was one to tip toe in order to keep the house quiet.

As he made his way down the street, he noticed no cars or foot traffic due to the early time of the day. He stepped into the local bakery, ordered his usual cup of coffee, and had a brief conversation with the clerk. She was a nice girl in her twenties with blonde hair, small build, and had a certain way about her. She handed him his coffee and a copy of the *Der Tagesspiegel* newspaper that he had been reading for as long as he could remember. He paid and then turned and was on his way.

He settled on a bus stop bench on the corner as he always did, due to the central location at the intersection, which gave him the mood of the city. This was his time to himself, when he could collect his thoughts, and think about the upcoming day.

He flipped open the paper and scanned the headlines. It was all bad news, as usual since the nuclear war. The world was in a bad way, but for some reason Germany had been spared, and was functioning at a low level of order.

He turned the pages until he got to Section Two, with several articles on politics and what was happening in the central government. The East and West German government had been consolidated into one federal body, and the Bundesrate (The German Regional States) had been disbanded, due to the emergency conditions.

There was a small article mentioning a new up and comer in the political world. His name was Rudi Bormann. He was from the Bavarian region of Germany, and had been drafted from the Christian Democratic Union due to his knowledge of politics, Germany's priorities to rebound from the emergency, and his casual manner.

As Karl read further into the article, it mentioned Bormann's ability to have different factions in the various parties, and government entities, talk to each other and get things done. He was young, energetic, and a great orator. In his most recent picture, he had dark brown hair combed to the side, and for some reason his face looked familiar. Karl searched his mind to place the face, but he could not.

He pondered the thought for a few moments, then finished his daily paper. For some reason, his mind was disconcerted. His anxiety level was increasing, but Karl did not know why. There was some long-ago seed planted in his mind, that he had seen this man before, but could not recollect where it had been.

He threw his coffee into the nearest trash container and made his way back home. He looked up in the sky; storm clouds were circling. It gave him an ominous feeling, but he just could not understand why.

## About the Author

Christian Mark is a graduate of Northeastern University with a Bachelor of Science degree. He worked in the life insurance industry for over 40 years. The author has had a lifelong love of writing and reading. Chris lives with his wife and family in southern Maine. He is also the author of *The Golden Child*.

CPSIA information can be obtained
at www.ICGtesting.com
Printed in the USA
LVHW110202200719
624757LV00001B/65/P